Settling

100 Snippets of Life
from a Mid-Century Woman

Deborah Williams Smith

Lost Lake **Folk Art**

SHIPWRECKT BOOKS PUBLISHING COMPANY

IN®
DIE

Minnesota

Cover design by Shipwreckt Books
Graphic cover illustration by Houchi

Dedication

With special dedication to my children, Syd, Jeff, Jeff's wife Kelli, and my stepdaughter, Jessica. With love to Lee and Elinor. And prayers and blessings for your future to Austin, Bailey, and Kiara, born on her Great-grandmother Imogene's birthday in 1998. To Mason, Kelsey, Cailie-Ann, Hayleigh and Willow: you are far away, but remembered each day. Kurtis Stephen, please look down on us all and be with us.

I dedicate this endeavor with a full heart to my late husband, Robert N. Oertle, and to his son, Robert D., who tragically perished in an accident three years ago. Blessings to Pam and her children.

From our Williams generation of only children, the late Patricia Williams McComas and the very recently departed Vernon L. Williams were special cousins. A loving nod to their sons, Steve Sypult, and Steve Williams, respectively. A warm dedication to some great wedding party pals, my maternal cousins, Nedra and Hope. Nedra's son, Brent is anticipating this book, while his sister Kathleen studies family ancestry during her sleepless hours as a mother of a young son with diabetes. Researcher Aunt Berneice, who was known as *Aunt Cotton*, lives on through daughter Janet. Precious thoughts of my late Aunt Golde, who allowed mud pie making. And to my light when Dad died, my late uncle, the Rev. Bernard Schroeder and his wife Milly, aka *Magna*.

A most special personal dedication is given to the late Roger Laverne Ramberg, who lived to see another day at Remagen. He surely taught lessons in not settling. Without his love, there would have been no confidence, no business done, no book. As we age, we are capable of drawing ever larger circles. I never stopped loving Roger after the 1980s, nor my husband, Bob (m. 1990) after his death in 2003. Both experiences only enhance my love for Stephen James Smith, the Englishman who stole my heart in 2006. This book, which he has so tirelessly edited, is ultimately for him.

I settle not.

Contents

Photos

Foreword

The sun chooses not to shine this morning, but this particular morning I most certainly wish to begin writing the foreword to my first book. Huge storms lashed the Gulf Coast last night, part of a system that tore through the midsection of the country and killed people in several states. I sit and think now how fragile and flashing life really is. My birth year is 1950, and such is my Twentieth Century blessing. Through my parents, I can think back to the early part of the century and then quickly forward to last night's pounding weather system. My body is aging now and feels the effects of such a storm, but I cherish the morning in the sunroom and the fact that there is another day to be lived.

Settling is about various forms of settling. Sometimes it just must be done and other times it can't be done. *Settling* is about people I have loved in one way or another. Although *Settling* is a work of fiction, its story lies very close to its truth. I have been blessed with a mother and aunts who were "preservers". Both the traditional shoe box and a CD with hand-written WWII letters, photos, Valentine's Day cards, and V-mail have been at my beck and call. There are letters on U.S. Navy stationery written by my father, and many, many letters written by a man who died on the way to the Bridge at Remagen, my uncle, Dall Roth, C-Company, 309th Infantry. Dall died one day in Germany, March, 1945, almost five years prior to my birth. He was my dad's best friend and also his brother-in-law. His life mattered to so many people and he is deserving of special mention here for paying the ultimate sacrifice for his country. And, may I say, as did his brother, George Roth. Dall and George died one day apart in Germany.

On Memorial Day, 2015, Stephen and I were able to attend a special service to honor Dall and George in Hume, Illinois. How moving it was! Thanks to veteran Bob Denbo of Hume. How thrilling to meet Ray Roth, George's son, and his family!

At age sixty-five, I have come to realize that my memory is now like a flashing camera, preserving snippets of life. If you are not yet sixty-five, you will remember people and events more clearly and acutely. But in the end, our life really is remembered in these camera flash moments that somehow get sorted into the "important bin" in our memories. And so, with this sorting of events that span from 1921 to 2015, now evolves the book to be told and to be shared.

The book began at my son's house. I talked with him – he ushered me to his theater room and I immersed myself in movies. I watched *The Bridge at Remagen* and *The Band of Brothers*. There I wrote and then read the first Snippets to Jeff. The first Snippet written was about receiving Dall back home. I remember a day in Paris in 2005 when Jeff's crystal eyes expressed what he had just seen during a visit to Normandy. He was thirty-three then. Thank you for your love of WWII, Jeff, and for helping me to start this book. Perhaps it will occupy a space in your sister's much overloaded, cherry-wood library. I can still see her reading books to you on the sofa as toddlers. I remember your curly head cuddled up to her red locks, two heads pressed together, reading together. Those camera flashes are still as vivid for me as the love is large.

"When it is all said and done," so the dying tell us, "all that matters is love, family, and friendship." The scorecards of life disappear and what matters stands before us. My memory is now full of these camera flashes of what is important after sixty-five years, and I have chosen to share some of them in these pages. The writing may appear clipped to some – I have an overriding desire to move the pace along – to camera flash through the years for a society that now lives in a tweeted world. As we cover these ninety-three years in one hundred snippets, I pray that you, the reader, are better able to see what is really important within your own life and families. Settle only when it is the right thing to do.

Deborah Williams Smith
Kitchen designer and soul-searched writer
Biloxi, Mississippi, 2015

Section One: Snippets 1-25
Doughboys, *Timberwolves* and the U.S. Navy (1921-1950)

1. The Pond, Fairview Farm
Sconce Estate, Vermillion County, Illinois, 1921
Harry and his older brothers, Dennis, Irvin, and Don

1. The Sconce Estate Fairview House 1919.

Harry was running as fast as his nine-year-old legs could carry him. He steered his body at an angle, bending towards the Boy Scout camp on the other side of the property line. The Sconce Estate pond almost touched the property line, and he had to run around the south end. He ran like a bat out of Hell, one of his brothers' favorite expressions. His older brother, Irvin, had screamed for him to go and get help. Irvin said Dennis was drowning and maybe Don as well. Harry had four older brothers; three were in the water. Harry did not stop until he was tugging on the arm of the scout leader.

"I think my brothers are drowning. Please come help us," Harry pleaded.

The scout leader scrambled with two other men and some life-saving equipment. By the time they all arrived back at the pond, it was too late to help Dennis. He had survived being a Doughboy in Europe, and he was a good swimmer. There was no

2. Fairview Farm entrance 1919.

explanation for this. Don had almost drowned trying to save Dennis, but he was going to survive. The other men helped to get Dennis' lifeless body out of the water. Harry thought of his mother, Alice, and he started to cry. He tried to hold the tears back, but he became ill. Harry was Alice's youngest child while Dennis had been her eldest, and the pain of this day would sear his soul. He had followed Dennis around; Dennis was Harry's hero.

2. Nellie
Vermillion County, Illinois, 1931
Harry and his family

Harry was a grown man now. He had young nephews who followed him about as if he were a hero. The family had gone quiet again. But now, the poor young lad. Poor young Vernon had lost his mother. It was as if Dennis had died all over again. Harry's sister-in-law, Nellie, had never been right, especially after young Vernon was born. Harry's older brother, Irvin, had tried to figure out what was wrong with his wife to no avail. Finally, she had taken her own life and left her son motherless. Vernon reminded Harry of himself. He would make sure he paid special attention to him whenever he could.

3. Ione in college, 1931.

Harry was in college at Eastern Illinois. His best friend, Dall Roth, was engaged to a woman named Magna Craig. Harry had seen Magna shopping with her sisters in Danville and could not help noticing how pretty they were, especially the sister whose arm was linked with Magna's.

"That would be Ione," Dall told Harry. "You must meet her, Harry, she is a doll!"

3. Blitzkrieg
Birmingham, England, 1941
Joanne and Jimmy

Joanne looked out of the window at the sky. She was six years old and again looking at a sky blackened with airplanes, shutting out the sun. She loved her older brother, Jimmy. He protected her when the sky turned to charcoal.

Birmingham, England, an industrial center, was a target. Eventually, she and Jimmy would be evacuated to the countryside. In the meantime, Jimmy would busy himself talking with the German POWs working on the roads. He was learning German out there with them, and Ernst, the nicest of the Germans, gave Jimmy his first harmonica.

Jimmy would one day become renowned as the classical harmonica virtuoso James Hughes, but for now, the unending blackness pounded and exploded their young minds into a resolute fear. Joanne was only six, a little blonde waif of a girl, but she felt herself becoming like steel inside. Good steel. Good Birmingham steel.

4. Dancing

Aragon Ballroom, Chicago, 1943

The gang: Magna and Dall, Ione and Harry, and their friends Fred and Willetta

Magna and Dall were snuggling together. They were all dancing at the Aragon dance hall – the whole dancing gang. Harry was always on top of his game when Dall was around, Ione mentally noted. The two men were best friends and they had married sisters; they were entwined forever. Dall was going to enlist in the army. His younger brother, Glenn, had been drafted and Dall wasn't going to let him go to war alone.

4. Harry and Ione, 1943.

The sisters, Magna and Ione, carried beauty gracefully. Dark hair was crimped over hazel eyes. There had been murmurs at college about Ione's bedroom eyes. Other men would be interested, but the sisters always took the moral high road. Ione already dreaded the thought of Dall leaving Magna to go to Europe, but they all presumed that is where he was headed. Harry was being drafted into the Navy. After nine years of marriage there were no children, and it was just as well.

"The world is in chaos," thought Ione, "and it is no time for children." Magna brooded over all of them, but she and Dall were also childless.

Tonight was about fun. Their good friend, Fred, had found a new woman after his nasty divorce. Fred was such a talker, lips always moving below bulbous nose, but he had clung to life quietly – an Irish Catholic ashamed of his divorce. Willetta, or Willie, as she was called, was so lovely. Ione liked her gentle spirit immediately. The night before, all of them had taken the train down to Cottage Grove Avenue to the opulent Trianon ballroom. The Trianon had its own radio station, WMBB, which stood for "World's Most Beautiful

Ballroom". Such was a Chicago tradition. For example, Chicago's most iconic radio station, WGN, chose call letters that stood for "World's Greatest Newspaper", because of its affiliation with the *Chicago Tribune*.

Tonight they were up on the north side where they lived – it was intimate, and the six of them would dance together for the last time. Fred was explaining to Willie that the ownership was the same at both the north and south side ballrooms. Older women, called hostesses, watched closely to make sure the women were conducting themselves in a ladylike manner; of course, Magna and Ione were never guilty of anything less.[1]

---

[1] Despite advertising themselves as the pinnacle of Democracy, both the Aragon and the Trianon, as well as the ballroom in Chicago's "White City" were completely segregated. Blacks were not allowed in. The big bands prevailed there. Jazz was found elsewhere in the city.

5. Harry's Basic Training

Great Lakes Naval Training Station, Chicago, June 20, 1943
Letter to Dall

After Harry was drafted into the Navy, he wrote the following letter to Dall, who served in the Army.

Dear Bub,

Well it was a shock I could hardly stand to get a letter from you and I could see the effort between every line, but I appreciated it. Well, I'm still kicking along and the Navy hasn't got me down yet, but it came pretty damn close a few times. I got quite a break although since I got here. I was appointed Company Clerk for our company. We have 118 men in the company.

I have an office and two assistants so I'm doing all right, eh Bub? I take care of a whole lot of the business of the company and have to tend to all the guards on duty in our company. It takes about 36 men to run the guards for each company.

Do you remember the hazards we saw the boys going over in the pictures? Well, I took that course this week and brother it was a tough one. We ran approximately two miles at the same time. We scaled a nine-foot wall - walked a twenty-five-foot rope with our hands, and a hell of a lot of other things. Plenty tough. We have learned to march rather well.

We really have to keep the old barracks spotless. They take steel wool every day and go over all the floors, dust everywhere, sandpaper the wood on the bunks, etc. I don't have to do any of the cleaning since I got this clerk's job. I work in the office and he has three fellows come in and clean up the office. That makes it a lot easier for me. He likes my work and told the boys I had it "on the ball" so I'm setting ok for a while anyway.

We don't get to have any visitors till July the 10th so you will probably be in Chicago too early to come out to see me.

We do all of our own washing and things really have to be clean. The Navy is really the cleanest life one could hope to live. We go to bed at 9:30 and get up at 5:30. Not bad hours. We have a nice bunch of boys and I know practically all of them now since I've been clerk.

My assistant clerk was a high school principal from Milan, Indiana, and has had six years' college work and has a master's degree. He will probably get a commission after boot training is over. I hope he does, for he is a very nice fellow and deserves a break. He is 36 years old.

Well Bub, I had better close for I have about five more letters to answer this afternoon and that will keep me busy for quite a while. Be seeing you one of these days. Goodbye.

Harry.

Because of their respective duties to the Army and the Navy, Dall and Harry saw each other only once more before Dall left for England. They embraced. Harry wiped back a tear. "Take care of yourself, Bub, you hear?"

5. Dall and Harry at 1348 Argyle St.

Dall and Harry's wives, the sisters Ione and Magna, continued their lives at 1348 Argyle St., Chicago.

6. V-Mail
European Theater, October 1944
Dall, Magna

Dall tried out the *Victory Mail*. He had no idea if it would actually be faster in getting his letter to Magna in Chicago. Known as V-Mail, it meant his letter was transferred to microfilm and reprinted smaller back home. The V-Mail arrived in a cute little brown envelope with an oval window.

6. Magna and Dall Roth before the war.

7. V-Mail.

When Dall was in training in England, he could not get used to the English currency. He wrote:

Mrs. Dall Roth, 1348 Argyle St., Chicago, Illinois.

England is a damp and cold country. And I have not seen a good looking woman since I left America.

Yours forever, Dall.

7. Discussing Marriage
Belgium, November 28, 1944
Dall, Laverne

8. Laverne, 1944.

Laverne was full of spunk. He would always do his duty and he was so proud of the ring he had given Barbara before he left Wisconsin. She said, "Oh Bud!" and kissed him appropriately, but he thought he saw disappointment in her eyes. He hoped not. Of all the girls back home, Barbara was the girl for him. She was smart; she had class, and he would not settle for any of the other girls. Her ginger hair sparkled around her face, and he loved her.

Dall Roth was Laverne's best friend of all the *Timberwolves* in the 311th Infantry, 78th Division – known as the *Lightning Division*. Dall was the elder statesman, like an older brother or uncle. Dall had told Laverne privately that he reminded him of his younger brother, Glenn. Mother Roth had died when Glenn was only six months old. Dall had three brothers fighting in the army, including Glenn. He also had a stunning raven-haired wife named Magna. The men shared photos of Barbara and Magna. One day Laverne and Barbara would be a happy couple like Dall and Magna. Laverne had given Barbara a hope chest before he left.

9. *Lightning Division* patch.

"What's it like to be married, Dall?" Laverne asked.

"Well, with a gal like Magna, it's a dream come true. She is like a CO and can do anything. I am

10. Christmas Day, 1944, in the Hürtgen Forest - the jeep had been hit by enemy fire an hour before this photo was taken.

a lucky man, that's for sure," stated Dall. "... and Frank Craig had the prettiest daughters in Champaign County."

Laverne contemplated. He was almost twenty-one years old and was usually known as Bud at home. He would save himself for Barbara and give her his all – right after they pushed back the Germans and won the war. So far, his life had been the army. He wanted to be back home making marriage plans with Barbara.

Laverne was a medic – he had to be tough and stay focused on the men. It seemed to help him that he was so highly strung. Dall was their cook and would joke and ask Laverne to take care of the "old men" first.

The 78th *Lightning Division* would become legendary. In future years, Laverne would proudly paste the Division's emblem on the license plate of his big black Lincoln town car.

11. Laverne washing his Jeep.

8. A New Rifle
Dall's letter from Belgium,
December 16, 1944

Dearest Magna,

Tomorrow is my birthday and I sure wish I was going to spend it with my wife. Sometimes I think I have lived longer than thirty-five years and then when I look back I wonder what has gone with the time. If I just knew that I would live another thirty-five with you honey, I would be satisfied. I sure hope by this time next year that I can be eating a birthday dinner with you.

When you and Harry and Ione sit down to the table, I sure hope that you all realize that you have a better dinner and a damn sight better place to be than where I am. Because the eats over here are not anything to talk about at all. And you know how well I like to eat. I sure would like to hear from home once more and get some of the boxes. And I sure as hell hope that they all have got cigs. in them. Because while I am writing this letter I am out of cigs. and would like to have one the worst way. Honey send me all that you can get a hold of. I told you once not to send any but things have changed since then.

Well I got my first rifle issued me today that I have had since I have been in the army. And I sure don't know a damn thing about it at all. It sure is hard to clean one up the first time.

12. Dall's Valentine to Magna. Note the G.I.'s *Lightning Division* shoulder patch.

To My Wife

This isn't much but the best I can do this time and the next time we will be together. I would like to be dressed like the picture above instead of the one below.

But there has been many a time I have studied your letters and read them with as much interest as the bottom picture.

With all the love I can send I say happy Valentines Day.

Love & Kisses   Dall.

13. Dall's Valentine's Day message.

We got electric lights put in today so I can write at night if I don't have time any other time. I have been cooking for the last three or four nights but starting Monday I have go to start in training with the rest of the fellows if I can keep up with them. Sometimes I wonder if I can be because my back has never been right since I hurt it that time. But I will try and if I can't they can't kill me for it.

Well honey I have just about run out of money again. We didn't get paid the first of the month and sometimes we run low. But they will probably pay us before long.

I really don't know what to write when I don't get any mail. But I know that I owe everyone a letter because you are all writing. I have got to write to Bernadine and Cotton both because they are pretty good about writing. I suppose by the time that you get this you will have been down home and had a big Xmas dinner and back to work again. That is just how far apart we are honey. But I think you can really believe me that no matter how far, I still love you and always will.

Well sweetheart, this is all for this time and when we get together again we have got a lot of time to make up just you and I. Please send the cigs. And tell Ione and Harry to send some if they can.

Every morning when I get up I think of you because you are just going to bed at that time so I tell you good night then. And now I say I love you again.

Dall

16

Magna tucked the Valentine into her pink satin handkerchief box. Ione had a matching box, and the sisters loved giving each other fancy handkerchiefs as gifts. Musing to herself, Magna languished in the moment of luxury she derived from tucking Dall's Valentine in amongst her treasured handkerchiefs. If only Dall were home, tucked away in bed with her.

9. Sleeping on the Steps
Italy, 1944
Alfred Smith, Glenn Roth

Alfred was war-weary. He just wanted to go home to Birmingham, England. As one of Montgomery's 8th Army, he had been involved in the defeat of Rommel at the Second Battle of El Alamein, having raced across Libya to the Tunisian border in February of 1943.

Alfred was a transport driver. He repeatedly took battle tanks to the front or delivered the Scottish Infantry to the front lines. He was a sitting duck in his lorry, but he managed to survive the constant treks back and forth.

Operation Husky had taken the island of Sicily and entered Italy at the southern toe of the boot. They were sent to the western side of the Apennine Mountains to assist the U.S. Fifth Army. The combined forces were successful! At one point, Alfred slept on the Spanish Steps in Rome. He talked to some Americans there, but could not remember names. He often thought of his friend, the lorry driver who drove the Amalfi Coast while sipping liquor from a tube. Alfred had been surprised that his comrade did not drive off the steep cliff roads as they snaked through the mountain passes. "Stone the crows!" Alfred would often exclaim.

The American, Glenn Roth, arrived at the Spanish Steps. He would eventually be wounded and sent home to Illinois. His three older brothers had enlisted because he was drafted. This knowledge ate away at his inner soul; he felt responsible.

10. Zinging Bullet
Luzon, Philippines, January 1945
Joseph

Joseph had a near miss with a Japanese bullet the day before. If he survived this hell-hole, every day from then on would be on borrowed time. His father had committed suicide. He would never do that, but the Japanese might do it for him. Joseph had a firebrand temperament and had driven for the Mob south of Chicago at one time. In those days, he had driven with a lead pipe under his seat. He was small, but wired tight and took no guff from anybody.

The 6th Army, under General Walter Krueger, had landed at the Lingayen Gulf. The men were well aware of the crucial aspect of this operation; the Philippines had to be re-taken.

Joseph thought about Lillian - the baby was due in a few weeks and he would not be there. She was the best thing that ever happened to him and he would not be there for her. He would either be dead or on this island or some other island. Well, he knew her parents would not let him down. Their entire German families lived close together on the far south side of Chicago. Her family, the Volckers, were well-known in those parts. Grandma Uhlaender-Volcker was a family force – they would surround the baby. Still, he was angry.

Joseph would end the military engagement with a Samurai sword in his possession.

11. Germany
January 19, 1945
Dall Writes Again

Well sweetheart, I will try and write a few more lines tonight because there will be days before long that I can't write. But not because I don't want to honey. I sure was surprised today when I got two letters from you. One Nov. 9 and 16th. In the first one you said you hadn't got the money I sent and in the other you had.

Well honey if I ever get paid again I will send it all home because I don't need any where I am at the present. None of the boys that I was with are with me; not one. They sure aim for a person to make new friends and you sure make them fast. I have taken a young boy named Laverne under my wing. He is from Wisconsin.

But my best and truest friend is you sweetheart - I mean that. I sure wish now that I had never had you send me any packages of any kind. Don't send me anything more not even cigs. Because all I am carrying now is what I have on my back and that is plenty.

I wrote the folks a letter today and I hope they don't think too much when I told them I was somewhere in Germany. And the same goes for you. I thought once I wouldn't even tell you. But after all honey you are the only one I have to tell my troubles to and I sure wish I was somewhere tonight to tell them to you. If I was where I could do that I wouldn't have any trouble at all!

Well honey we just had some popcorn. One of the boys got a box and it sure tasted good. Well sweetheart tell Harry and Ione that I said hello and I still say that Harry is lucky by being in the Navy and tell him to stay as close to home as he can just as long as he possibly can. Because it sure isn't so nice over here as it is mapped out to be.

Well sweetheart, I am going to have to go on guard and I sure don't like it a bit either, but someone has got to do it. So I say good night to the sweetest wife in the world and all I am waiting for is to get back to her and spend the rest of my days with you. I love you honey more every day and hope that you are the same way and we will have a honeymoon again when I get home. Good night sweetheart and sweet dreams. Love to you. Dall.

Dall finished writing and turned to watch his best buddy, Laverne. Laverne leaned over their friend, Ed Malouf, inspecting Ed's leg wound one more time. Ed had been hit by shrapnel in the forest, diving through the snow into a two man underground dugout while taking incoming fire. His feet did not make it into the hole in time. Had it not been for thick boot leather and a heavy buckle, the shrapnel would have crushed his bone. As it was, Ed's boot stopped the shrapnel just above the bone. Ed seemed to have recovered, and continued carrying his 60mm, M2 mortar which weighed in at forty-two pounds. Ed was only about one hundred forty-two pounds himself, but strong and up to the job. Ed was a character, bright and forceful. Ed's unit awarded him the *Royal Cabbage Leaf Award* for carrying eight eggs in his helmet for two days, leaving his head unprotected. In the end, Ed said he should have been awarded a capital *S* for stupid. But Laverne and Dall knew he was anything but that!

12. First Army and *The Bridge*
Remagen, Germany, March 1945
Laverne and Dall

Laverne's exhaustion permeated his inner soul. He was thin; he looked younger than he was. He was ordinary-looking in one way, but he had a sly, sexy look that could catch women off-guard, given the chance. The 311th Infantry, the *Timberwolves*, had held their line in the forest that winter, but men's faces pierced what little sleep came Laverne's way. He did his best - his best to patch them and get them pulled back. Some were half-men, and Laverne watched others empty their lives in the forests. They had been attached to the 8th Infantry Division in the Hürtgen Forest. As a medic, Laverne worked under the direction of Major Florides.

Being a medic was heart-shredding, tough work. On the east side of the Roer River, the advance had been extremely rough, fraught with hardship. The road along the river was heavily mined and unusable by the 311th. The hills rose high above the river, too steep even for the M29 *Weasel*, a terrain vehicle built by Studebaker. The medics had improvised at times, using old doors and bed springs to create the litters on which to move the wounded. In addition, relay stations were necessary to get the men pulled back.

The *Timberwolves* had secured the Schwammenauel Dam, a huge victory. They had pressed on towards the Rhine. It was not easy. Kesternich had been a building-to-building fight. The snow was waist-deep into Simmerath where the 309th had cut the supply line to the Panzer division. Some men reported the enemy ran, helmets off, hands in the air. Still it was serious business. The G.I.s experienced the smell of victory and kept pushing east. The desire to cross the Rhine and ram deep into the Fatherland was fixed in their minds. Circling forward, the 311th Infantry served to protect the division on the south side as the troops closed on the town of Remagen. Laverne knew, like everyone, that the end of the war was near. The First Army, like the Third Army, would continue the push toward Berlin. Laverne was descended from German musicians and architects; he spoke German, and he had sadness that these were the circumstances of coming to Germany.

That evening, Laverne noticed Dall taking in Magna from her nearly worn-out photo. Dall had kept a letter from his brother-in-law Harry in the Navy, but it stayed in his pocket as he talked to Magna. It had just been their twelfth anniversary, and Dall wanted his wife. He wanted some of Magna's special fried chicken, dipped in cornflakes, followed by him helping with the dishes for a change. Then they would go to bed like the old married couple they were … and it would be grand. Like a honeymoon. One week had elapsed from their positions at the Roer River to the new position at the Rhine.

The men awoke to a change of plans that laced even the most experienced of them with shock and alarm. The orders were to take the bridge at Remagen as an entrance to the Führer's Reich. The Germans had it wired, and only hell could have looked more deadly. A widespread rumor held that the bridge was about to be blown by the enemy – at four p.m. On the east bank, curious young spectators took position to see the bridge blown, but most citizens hid in fear on the east side of the Rhine River.

Laverne felt ill as he envisioned the spray of blood to come. Orders had waffled, as the area really was not well-suited for a largescale crossing and there was no buildup of supplies. The army had not planned to cross the Rhine on the Ludendorff Bridge at Remagen. But there stood the bridge. Shortly before four, Americans started across the bridge. The Germans had blown a hole about six feet deep and twenty feet wide at the entrance. Engineers followed infantry, cutting wire and kicking explosives off the bridge into the Rhine. The Germans, who had been delivered fewer explosives than requisitioned, and faultier, attempted to blow the bridge. The detonators failed. A German officer ran out to make a manual attempt and there was an explosion. The bridge heaved up and down, but when the smoke cleared, there it stood. Fortunately, the Germans had planked over one of the railroad lines on the bridge to move their own troops; more fortifications were required. The engineers scrambled and smoke machines were garnered from every possible point to screen their activities.

March 8th, the first day of the battle for the bridge, the Luftwaffe came out in force. First Battalion made it across. Then Dall's company, the 311th, crossed the river under a ferocious air attack.[2] In one week, the American troops in Remagen expanded from a single battalion to four divisions.

Just a few miles up the river, six-year-old Rosalie stood staring. Ethnically Italian, Rosalie was born just twenty miles from the Ludendorff Bridge. Her parents told her to stay in the basement of her three-hundred-year-old house, but she just had to go outside. She saw a sky as thick with airplanes as the basement was thick with old stone.[3] The Luftwaffe was on its way to attack the bridge.

Under a spray of bullets, Laverne watched soldiers far out on the bridge, about five hundred feet, prone, not moving. He knew Dall was one of them. There was no way he could get way out there to the old man now. Under the air attack, Laverne drove his jeep onto the bridge to retrieve an officer nearer to the approach, bullets whizzing past him. One man retrieved, then out to get another, and another.

Eventually, he had to stop and attend to the wounded – too much blood. He blinked back tears, sweat and blood that soaked his uniform. He could not work fast enough. He pushed himself, challenging his mind and hands to work ever faster. Somehow, Laverne just knew Dall was dead. He worked on steadily, yelling and giving instruction for whomever would help him stop the font of blood from erupting into a cascade of death.

The bridge would remain another ten days before it would drop into the Rhine, taking the lives of twenty-eight American engineers. But on March 8th, the battle continued. Laverne lost track of how many men he helped pull back and treat. In the end, Dall's body lay next to his feet and Laverne kneeled to search Dall's lifeless face for one last word of wisdom. Dall had been dapper. He usually came out of battle looking like he just stepped from a shower. Not this

---

[2] Part of *Operation Lumberjack*, the battle for the Ludendorff Bridge began with the First Army, 14th Tank Battalion. Able Company of the 27th Armored Infantry Battalion, crossed first, then B-company, then C. German-born Lt. Karl H. Timmerman, twenty-two years old, along with his Sgt., Alexander A. Drabik, of Holland, Ohio were the first two men across the bridge and into history. No invader had crossed the Rhine since the time of Napoleon until that moment.

[3] Based upon the memories of LRF of Minneapolis, as told to E. Hallowell. LRF was born of Italian parents in 1939 at Andernach am Rhein. Her father was head of the Red Cross efforts in the area. She watched the bombs drop like, "eggs from the sky," from her second floor bathroom window.

day. Dall was gone from this world. Only his shell remained. Laverne thought of Magna Roth for a second, but pushed the pain backwards.

By March 9th, sixteen battalions, including the 78th Division, had crossed the Rhine. Laverne and his *Lightning Division* fellows were fully engaged on the east side of the Rhine, to the north. The allies had crossed into the heart of the Third Reich on the Ludendorff Bridge at the village of Remagen. By March 13th, the *Lightning Division* had taken Honnef on the east side, cutting part of the Autobahn. Laverne took a German luger off a dead German officer and obtained permission to keep it. He then soberly wondered if he would ever see Barbara again. For once, Laverne was fairly quiet.[4]

---

[4] Lt. General Courtney Hodges, who took over the 1st Army from Bradley, was soon to be made a four-star general. Only he and General Walter Krueger, who served in the Pacific, made history by being the only men to rise from Private to General.

13. Fruit Farm and the Future
Treasure Island, San Francisco, 1945
Harry and Ione

Ione loved Illinois, especially Chicago. She would always want to stay there. Harry was a burst of life in San Francisco and had taken her up to see some of his relatives with a fruit farm north of the city. Sonoma was heavenly and his old aunt and uncle had no children to leave it to as an inheritance. Ione could read Harry's thoughts – he was a natural businessman and organizer. She would never leave Illinois. As soon as Harry shipped out to Pearl Harbor, she would return to Chicago and live with Magna at 1348 Argyle St. She would get a new job – she was pretty organized herself.

14. Dall and Magna with his brother George and George's wife Bernadine at 1348 Argyle before going overseas.

Things changed quickly when word of Dall's death reached them. Ione clung to Harry, shaking with fear. It was unthinkable that her Magna would go through this agony. Ione released Harry and sat down. She held her pretty head in her hands, the feeling of marbles banging together inside of it. To make matters worse, Dall's brother, George, pictured above, was killed in action the day before Dall, leaving Bernadine a widow with two young boys, Donald and Roy.

Magna went down home. For once, she needed others to care for her, just for a little while. She had known deep in her heart and soul that Dall would not come back to her. Ione decided to go back down home as well. She would get a job at Chanute Air Force base. She could breathe easier in Illinois and Magna would need her.

The long train ride back to Illinois was very difficult for Ione. She felt very alone without Harry and Magna. Other passengers noticed her, her all-blue outfit, her favorite color; her smoky eyes teasingly visible under her fashionable hat. Ione's thoughts were constantly on Magna and Dall. She wondered how he had died and if he died quickly. She knew Magna was having these same thoughts. Magna's instincts had been an accurate foreshadowing. Only Dall's war-battered remains would return, and even not that for a while. Ione would do all she could to be there for Magna in her time of need.

Ione was already acquainted with loss, having lost three brothers. Ned Craig had died of rheumatic fever. Harlan died in a car accident. Ione had seen the accident site. And Kent died from a blow to the head four days after falling on ice. Ned was young and single when fever took him. Harlan left an orphan baby. Kent, poor dear Kent, was just a newlywed when he died. Their father, Frank Craig, was dead, but that did not have meaning for Ione. She had reason not to love her father. Ione didn't like most men. One man had tried to get friendly on the train ride. She put him right in his place.

14. Harry's Letter to Magna
Pearl Harbor, Hawaii, 1945
Harry, Magna, Ione

On the starry Friday night of July 20, 1945, Harry wrote to his sister-in-law:

I hope by now Magna that things are better with you. I know that this thing is something that it will take a mighty long time to overcome and doubt if it will be possible in a lifetime to rebuild the things that were torn from us in such a short time, but it seems that is one thing that we must do - but I know it is mighty hard to do.

I have been getting word right along from Ione as to how you were feeling and what you have been doing and have been glad to hear that you have been feeling better. I do not know what your plans are for the future yet Magna, but I have been trying to map out a few things that I hope to do when I once more get back home. You know - just sort of dreaming around on the possibilities and I believe that when the time comes that we can get into some business that will work out and if you have not decided on anything else by that time, I have certainly planned for you being with us in anything that we do.

It is very hard to express in so many words Magna, the way I feel about this whole thing. I know I have lost the best friend I ever had in this world, when we lost Dall in Germany, and I just cannot bring myself to believe the truth of the whole thing. Life has been so mixed up ever since. I had just left when it all happened but have spent many a night lying and thinking about things. I enjoyed the days in Chicago with the three of you more than I had enjoyed life in a long time and we had many gorgeous times, times that we will never forget. I know if he could, he would still tell us to do the best and not give up the fight for the things that we always dreamed about.

Of course, we know that it will never be the same but the thing left for us to do is to pull together the things we have and do our best. Magna, I want you to always remember that there is nothing in this world you could not ask of me and get for I think you are one of the grandest girls on earth and this should not have happened to you, but it did so we will win this battle yet. If it had been the other way around and Ione was left, I know that I would not have had to worry any, if worrying goes with the rest, for I know Dall would have certainly done anything he could. He was my best friend on earth, Magna, without any doubt about that.

Harry.

15. Nephew in Paradise
Pearl Harbor, Hawaii, 1945
Harry

On one hand, Harry felt lucky to be alive, but he was incredibly sad as well. It still seemed like an unending nightmare that his brother-in-law and best friend Dall was gone. As for Harry, he felt guilty now that he would be sitting out the war in relative paradise. He was thirty-three years old and most of the guys were younger than Harry. Sure, a war was on - but as an older draftee, he continued his clerk's job. He dealt with all the personnel in and out of Pearl Harbor. As usual, he was organized and efficient.

Harry was so easy-going, and it was a good thing. His gorgeous wife got a bit nervous about things. Something had made her a bit jumpy, even when he touched her. Harry's fair skin had burned in the tropical sun and his thoughts wandered from Ione to his Irish mother - she had passed on her fair skin to Harry. He was her baby and she was a naturally warm woman. Ione ... well, she tanned up nicely. Frank Craig had the most beautiful daughters in Champaign County.

Dall had been his best friend in this world; and he had such affection for his sister-in-law Magna. God, he wished they were all at the Aragon Ballroom dancing. It sure would beat that exhibition of the young sailors the night before – all dancing in grass skirts and braziers. The four of them would never dance the Aragon again, he thought sadly. Those days were over. Harry loved to dance and hoped he might again.

Harry was reviewing the list of incoming personnel when he noticed something incredible. His young nephew Vern was about to arrive by boat! Vern was only eighteen years old, the only son of Harry's older brother Irvin, known as Big Boy due to his 6'6" height. Vern plus Jack and Conrad, Harry's sisters' sons, loved Uncle Harry

Harry remembered the day his older brother Dennis, *The Doughboy,* drowned in the pond at Sconce estate where their father worked as caretaker. Harry was just a little shaver of nine years the day he followed his older brothers to the pond. He could not get help fast enough to save his hero Dennis. Harry had identified with Vern because Vern was just a kid when his own mother died.

Harry started drawing up papers to get Vern off the boat as soon as it hit harbor because there was no shore leave planned for the inbound sailors.

Harry would put him on the back of the motorcycle and show him paradise. It was a long way from Illinois, the Sconce estate and the pond. Meanwhile, Vern hustled to the top deck. He had no idea why he'd been paged until he saw the most unimaginable thing, his Uncle Harry standing next to a ship's officer waving papers. Vern blinked, wondering if he was dreaming. He didn't know until then that Harry was stationed at Pearl Harbor!

16. A Baby as Spring Breaks
Chicago Heights, Illinois, 1945
Lillian and her son Richard

Lillian was a strong woman in her own right, smart as a whip when it came to technical matters and finances. She had steely, gray-blue eyes, layered with intelligence. In addition, she had bundles of Volcker family support for herself and the only child she would ever have. Her husband, Joseph, was serving in the Philippines and she prayed that he would live to see their child, Richard, who had arrived on March 3rd into the bosom of a family who would treat him as a little prince. Growing up, he would feel secure, even when he stole pies from his Grandmother's window. A cooling pie was fair game for him.

But for now, Richard was an infant who was told his Daddy was a photograph on the bureau. His crib was in his mother's room at Grandma Volcker's, but he had plenty of visits from his young aunt. Bethany was only six years old and loved this new addition to the Volcker family. Lillian was Lutheran; she prayed diligently for the safe return of her husband, Joseph.

17. Victory in Europe
Germany, 1945
Laverne and Erika

Laverne's mind was both musical and mathematical; normally it absorbed quite well. In recent weeks, however, sounds and speech sometimes seemed to bounce off. The *Lightning Division* had made their way to Marburg by V-E Day. The 311th Infantry now became the occupiers of a devastated Germany. They set up headquarters in the town of Grebenstein. Colonel Chester Willingham utilized a large house as his headquarters. Laverne saw things he would not be able to discuss in the future. He was soon tapped as an interpreter. Laverne spoke both German and Polish from his days in the Wisconsin farming communities. He was a natural linguist.

In Grebenstein, Major Joe Lipsius joined the 311th. Joe was thinking of going on to Japan, but just then the war was over in the Pacific. He wound up editing the history of the 311th, a project undertaken by six G.I.s down in Fülda. Laverne liked Joe and knew he would do a good job with the editing and recording of all that had happened.

15. First Sergeant and Laverne with wild boar.

One day, Laverne's first sergeant invited him to go hunting. They came back with a wild boar!

Laverne felt alive again in some moments. Though fraternization was officially prohibited, enlisted soldiers like Laverne were housed with German families.

Next door to Laverne's hosts lived a family with a daughter named Erika. Thankful, really, that the war was over, and thankful for the sacrifices made by American soldiers, Erika was drawn to Laverne. There was no language barrier for Laverne, and anyway, her language was international in its flavor and she was hauntingly a woman in every sense of the word. Laverne could not resist her, not one bit. She invited him into her room when she was home alone with an almost desperate look in her blue eyes. Her blonde hair lay in waves against her exposed breasts; he was incapable of stopping himself. His emotions were both raw and alive; her passion undeniable. Erika called him Buddy, an endeared form of his usual

16. Laverne crouches near the wild boar.

Bud, and in their most private moments she would call out his name, "Buddy, Buddy …"

Thoughts of Barbara and America seemed so remote now. With Erika, he felt alive again. He poured all the emotion of The Bridge and the war into his lovemaking and he could tell she was in love with him. He had to be honest with Barbara; he wrote her about Erika. His nerves were shattered and his mind splintered.

17. Laverne and his Jeep on
V-E Day, 1945.

18. Broken Engagement
Chicago, 1945
Barbara and Her Sister

Barbara was indignant. Her penetrating eyes flashed. How could he do this to her? At first opportunity, she had been forgotten. Fiancée indeed. All the things he had said to her were now tossed aside. She wrote quickly to Laverne to break off their engagement. Hope chest indeed. She could do better than to be treated like this. Her sister Doris agreed. Swift action had been taken and the ring was gone.

Barbara had her reservations anyway. She was educating herself; she wanted to reach a high level in nursing. Really, she imagined herself with a professional man. Not a guy off the farm whose only credentials were the U.S. Army. Sometimes the way Laverne looked at her made her very uncomfortable.

19. Christmas Week
San Diego, California, 1945
Harry

Harry was at the Trianon-Pacific Ballroom, 11th and Broadway, San Diego, right before Christmas. He was on his way; he would make it back to Chicago eventually. For now, it was a good time out with the guys. Harry didn't drink much – too many episodes when his mother Alice called him to pull his drunken sister Gladys out of bars had cured him of wanting much drink – but a beer here and there was appreciated. Besides, Ione hated drinking and the smell of beer on a man's breath. He rarely drank around her. He thought of Alice now. She was getting older and being kept by his sober sister, Eleanor. Alice never thought Harry did anything wrong. Of course, in his youth, he had been out by the barn smoking with the other boys; Alice just did not know.

There was a great atmosphere, the war being over. Japan had surrendered on September 2nd. The men were happy and a sense of real freedom and strength surged through their entire generation. They had done their duty, and they had done it well. If only Dall had made it through, thought Harry, everything would be perfect. Harry frowned to himself, as George Roth had not made it through either. Of the four brothers who all went to Europe, two were killed and two returned home wounded. When Dall and George were killed, their father, Chester, was sent a letter asking him to choose between remaining brothers Harold and Glenn as to who would come home immediately. Chester Roth could not make that choice, but Harold chose for him. Harold had almost enough points to come home anyway, so Glenn was sent home. He was the youngest.

Harry reflected on these things as he enjoyed the one beer. The islands had been beautiful, even under war circumstances. Harry had managed to do a good tour of the islands on leave prior to his departure from Pearl Harbor. Ione's cousin, Dale, who was in the army, had visited and the two men toured around together. Harry was older than most of the guys. He had stayed true to Ione, although there was one evening it had not been easy. Ione never relaxed when she was with him; she was always a stiff, absent lover. This bothered Harry, but he was a good man; he rose above it and settled for what he had. He knew Ione loved him. He had taken her away from an arranged marriage, and she had been so happy then. Harry wanted to bring Ione back to Hawaii someday under different circumstances. For now, he was just happy to be stateside and closer to home. Still, he wanted Ione and Magna to come back out to California and see the farm in Sonoma. Harry always wanted more from life.

18. Harry, second from left, Dec. 23, 1945, San Diego.

20. Christmas Week
Germany, 1945
Laverne "Buddy" and Erika

"Buddy, Buddy," she called out as the train began crawling away. "Verlass mich nicht!" [Don't leave me.] There were so many bodies. Erika's voice faded fast from his earshot and he hung his head in despair, perhaps shame. If only she had not become pregnant, although the thought of life going on after his baptismal immersion in death soothed his shell-shocked soul. Laverne believed marriage was verboten [forbidden].

Bud unfolded Barbara's letter. He would become Laverne, his given name, a man's name. He would see her again stateside and convince her again to marry him. He was headed straight to her sister's place in Chicago as soon as he was separated at Fort Sheridan. Germany had to release him before his mind played more tricks. He cried. He had to stroke just hard enough to get his head above water. He closed his eyes and there it was in an instant. The Bridge – that damned bridge – lying at the edge of his sanity. Even Rheinwiesenlagers, [concentration camps] and making love with Erika had not wiped out the memories of the bridge. He thought about Dall and Magna Roth. He wanted what they had, even if only for twelve years. He would not settle for less.

21. Photography
England, 1946
Alfred and Joanne

Alfred made it home to Birmingham, England, his home city, in one piece. He had been a Desert Rat and had slept on the Spanish Steps in Rome. His lorry had made many trips without it resulting in his demise. Once home, Alfred worked at the store for Birmingham and Blackburn Steel. He had been disappointed in the romance department and spent many spare hours honing his skills as a photographer. Alfred had dark hair. He was handsome.

Joanne was eleven years old and so happy to be living a normal life again without the airplanes darkening the sky. She was home from the countryside, back in Brum. She was bright, and excelled in her school work. Music filled the home. Her older sister Olga was brilliant at the piano, and Jimmy was becoming ever so good at the harmonica. Everybody loved to sing and listen to big band music from America.

22. Homecomings
Chicago, 1946
Laverne, Harry and Joseph

Laverne arrived to a frigid Chicago and eagerly left Fort Sheridan. Barbara had agreed to see him. Doris, her sister, had encouraged Barbara - after all, he had just risked his life to fight for his country. Barbara was tearful that he had not waited for her, humiliated that he had found another. She felt she had much to offer any man, yet it had not been enough for Laverne. Barbara wondered, did he love her? Did he love Erika?

"Look, Barbara," he said, "I just got carried away because I was alive. You have no idea what it was like over there or the things I saw. I think I just wanted to make sure I was living and breathing, and I just got carried away. I am so sorry to have hurt you. As soon as I wrote the letter, I knew it was all wrong. I felt guilty, but I never stopped loving you, Barbara. You are the one for me. It was crazy over there and for a short time I could not even remember what it was like to be home." In the end, Barbara saw things his way. He could be very emotional and persuasive. Laverne would not ever tell her about the baby. He put Erika and the baby in a mental box, and locked it with a key.

Harry hit Maxwell Street as soon as he returned. It was flooded with men needing clothes, and he could not wait to be a civilian again. Ione met him in Chicago, and he was so happy to see her that his grin would have drawn in any woman.

Ione was so very relieved to see her green-eyed, blonde husband. He was home. Ione languished in his arms; one of the few times she really relaxed with Harry. She was so happy that she forgot to be tense. Harry had a job waiting down home and they all wanted to be there for Magna.

Joseph did not die in the Philippines. He made it back to his steel-eyed Lillian and little baby boy, Richard, south of Chicago. Richard looked at him with those same eyes. It took Richard a while to warm to his father and he did not like Lillian paying attention to her husband. That was okay with Joseph for the moment; they had a lifetime to be father and son. Joseph was excited to start his life anew. He would work hard and show Lillian that she had made the right decision when she agreed to marry him. He had been driving for the Mob in earlier days, making runs up and down Illinois Route One. Lillian had put an end to that. No more Dixie Highway for him.

23. Dall's Return
Orchard Field, Chicago, 1947
Ione and Magna

Fall was absent that year in Chicago. Summer had quickly yielded to winter. Ione, shivering, glanced once more at her eldest sister Magna and wondered how Magna remained resolute. They stood waiting at Orchard Field, Ione's shuddered stance, however, not a reflection of the Chicago weather.

Ione wondered to herself, what if Harry's body lay in that casket? Ione knew she would not be like Magna if that had been the case. Yet Magna's strength strained at its very edges as they waited to receive Dall's remains from Germany. The war had been over for two years. That bridge – that awful bridge – had changed everything. Ione and Harry, Magna and Dall, they were supposed to all grow old together. Now those dreams were as obliterated as the sun and there was no fall, just ghostly chill. They would have to settle.

24. Wedding Bells
Wisconsin, November 1947
Laverne and Barbara

Laverne was getting dressed for his wedding. He had not settled for any other girl. He had convinced Barbara they were meant to be together. He had that sly look on his face and he was looking forward to the wedding night. He cut his sandy brown hair short. It would always be that way. He liked things neat and tidy.

While he served in the Army, his parents moved from the farm to the town, and he had to track them down upon arrival. He stopped to ask somebody their whereabouts, and it turned out they were just across the street! Laverne had crossed to the house and appropriately into the arms of his older brother, Truman. God, it was good to be home. Truman was his best friend.

Barbara was beautiful, just as Laverne had imagined her, but better. He could not wait for the honeymoon. Barbara was walked into her parents' living room slowly supported by her father. Her ginger hair was a contrast to the white veil. Doris and Truman were in attendance, both happy that this day had finally arrived. Laverne saw flashes of Erika – moments of passion he could not wipe away – passion that let go of so much pain. The baby would be over a year old now. He had told nobody in Wisconsin about the baby and he worked hard now to push Erika out of his thoughts and to think only about making things good for Barbara. He wanted to have all that passion, but he wanted to have it with Barbara and raise a family with her in his home state of Wisconsin.

Laverne was a natural-born salesman. He knew he could always make money selling things. It didn't matter what they were. He was high-strung and a little obsessive. Army training and the war had only intensified those natural tendencies.

25. Night Emergency
Mercy Hospital, Champaign County, Illinois, 1950
Magna, Ione, Harry, and Diane

Magna rushed to the hospital after being shocked awake in the middle of the night by Harry's phone call. Harry and Ione had taken their daughter Diane to the hospital. Harry himself had awakened with a start, somehow knowing that his six-week old baby's cold was serious.

"Please, God, not another loss! No, no, no," Magna prayed as she entered the waiting room, anxious to give her support. She had never seen two more worried or sad people in her life. Ione threw herself in Magna's expectant arms, sobbing. Harry was quiet, numb and speechless.

"They hurried away with our baby, Magna," Ione cried, "and we have to stay here."

In 1949, Ione underwent minor surgery at the Christie Clinic hoping finally to conceive the child she and Harry so desperately wanted. The procedure worked, but Ione would never become pregnant again. Due to her difficulties, a caesarean section was scheduled for March 16th, but Ione went into labor early and gave birth to Diane the natural way on the 15th, just two days after Harry turned thirty-eight. Conveniently, Diane arrived on his afternoon off from managing the grocery store. During childbirth, Ione had a terrible reaction to the anesthetic. When the nurses told her she had a baby girl with a round head, Ione imagined the baby's head was deformed and was not right for several days.

Ione suffered from post-partum depression, a nearly impossible situation made even worse for her when Harry rushed her and the baby to Mercy Hospital.

She was worried sick when the doctor entered and announced, "Mr. and Mrs. Williams, I think you are very lucky parents tonight. I believe your daughter will survive, but she has pneumonia in both lungs. She would have been dead in her crib by morning."

Ione collapsed. Harry and Magna gently urged her back into her seat. Harry thought his mind would explode. Baby Diane was his entire world already, even at only six weeks. He had never been so happy. They would have to be even more diligent as parents. Nothing could ever happen to Diane. He would tell Ione that they both had to be the most alert parents in the world. He knew this was his only shot at being a father. He would do everything he could for Diane. Everything.

Harry finally found his voice. "Can we see her now, doctor?"

"Yes, come this way please."

Magna stood to watch them go. She had recently married a widower with four children herself. This next generation was presenting its challenges, but hopefully the dark days were now over. She had lost three brothers, two accidentally, and a husband. With only one brother left, the four sisters would need to stand strong, and she was the oldest. She took stock. Diane was the youngest of all the grandchildren in the family. There were twelve of them now, plus Magna's four new, ready-made children. She viewed herself as the matriarch, and so did everybody else. Her father had died long ago, but she would need to get word to her mother about Diane. She prayed Goldie would not berate Ione about the pneumonia.

Section Two: Snippets 26-48
Settling-in (1951-1981)

26. The Reality of Life
Wisconsin, 1951
Laverne and Barbara, Janet

Laverne and Barbara had been married almost four years, and as happy as they were ever going to be, when Janet was born. Passion never really erupted between them. Barbara had too many lovemaking rules for Laverne to keep track of. And he just wasn't geared that way. It was like trying to put a Ferris wheel into a gymnasium. It just didn't work between them, which really shocked Laverne. He thought it would all be automatic. He simply was unprepared for her repression. Well, he loved the thought of being a dad. Maybe motherhood would change things. They were a family now.

Barbara was college educated. He was not. His education had come in Germany. Sometimes, Laverne would take out his German Luger war souvenir and look at it. In years to come, he would notice it was the same as the one James Bond carried in the movies. Hell, he watched the movies for the women, though, not the Luger. His most prized possession from the War was his Bronze Star. And, ruefully, he admitted his most prized memories were of the young German woman, Erika.

27. Wedding Bells in the Midlands
Birmingham, England, 1952
Joanne, Clive, Alfred

Joanne was eighteen and a true English Rose for her beloved Clive on their wedding day. She imagined the wonderful life they were going to have. An adult now, the sky no longer black with the sun shut out, she felt smart and strong. And she was. She was wafer-thin, but you could see the strength in her.

Joanne and Clive hired a photographer for their modest wedding. Alfred was his name. Alfred made her feel beautiful for the photographs - the way he admired her dress and hair. She hoped Clive would be pleased with the photography. Joanne's older sister, Olga, played the piano and was an accomplished musician for the event. Her older brother, James Hughes, would contribute musically as well, and it would be very special.

Less than a year after the wedding, Joanne, beaten and bruised, found the strength to leave her abusive husband. She went home to her parents' house. It wasn't long until a family friend, Alfred the photographer, found out about her circumstances. Alfred was angry that such a fine woman had a horrific start in life. He vowed he would treat her differently.

28. The Wagon Wheel Room and Croquet
Waukegan, Illinois, north of Chicago, 1955
Diane, Fred and Willie, Harry and Ione, Magna and Bernard

Diane loved visiting Fred and Willie in the suburbs north of
Chicago. They were from her parents' old dancing gang. Diane lived
with her parents, Harry and Ione, on a beautiful tree-lined street in
a city west of Chicago. They left down home when Harry was
transferred to manage another grocery store. With Harry's blonde
hair crowning her head, she fit in visually with the Swedish
neighborhood.

Often, her parents would take her to the northern suburbs of
Chicago to see their old friends. Diane loved it there. Four parents;
she was treated very well. The house was large and well-appointed,
as Fred made a good living in insurance. Diane's favorite things
about the house were the linoleum floor in the recreation room – it
was like a big wagon wheel – and the bathroom doorknob was clear
and faceted with a rose inside. The rose was yellow, and it always
reminded her of Harry singing to her, for he loved to sing *The
Yellow Rose of Texas*. Both of these items fascinated the young Diane.

Willie and Fred were talking to Harry and Ione about Florida.
Well, Fred did most of the talking. He really wanted to move there
and tried trying to talk Harry into going into real estate in a place
called Boca Raton. But Ione would never leave Illinois.

Sometimes Harry and Ione would take Diane down home. Diane
had eleven cousins on Ione's side, all older. In addition, she had six
cousins on Harry's side, all older by far. The first two years of
Diane's life, the family had lived down home. Diane's paternal
cousin, Sheryl, Don's only child, was sixteen years old when Diane
was born; she was her first babysitter. Sheryl was close to her Uncle
Harry and her nose was out of joint a bit at this new arrival when
she was sixteen. But Sheryl could see herself in this baby. She loved
her immediately. Baby Diane even had green eyes.

 Most of the time when they went down home, they spent time
with Ione's family. Her younger sister had three girls – just stair

51

steps above Diane. Diane always wanted to go there and play with Nedra, Dana, and Cara. Cara, being the youngest, was the logical choice of playmate. But in adult years, Nedra would become near and dear. Nedra was named for Ned Craig, the uncle who had perished from rheumatic fever and left Magna as eldest sibling. Oddly, in later years, Nedra's eldest son would resemble Ned Craig.

19. Harry reading to Diane in his favorite chair.

The eldest of the next generation was Cousin Shirley's first child, Hope, who followed Diane around intently. Hope, too, would be important in later years. Hope's Grandpa Bob was the only surviving brother for the four sisters, Magna, Betty, Ione, and the younger Golde, named for their mother. Great times happened at Aunt Magna's house. She had a huge dining room, center of the house, and she served up fried chicken to as many family members as showed up – and don't forget about her pies! Aunt Magna had an interesting chime installed at the bottom of the stairway; Diane never knew why it was actually there, but she loved to bong the chimes and make melodies.

Aunt Magna's stepson had married and lived close to Harry and Ione to the far west of Chicago. Magna's new husband, Bernard, and his son, Jack, loved to take Harry on in a game of croquet when they came up from down home. Harry usually won and everybody would become frustrated with his tactics. Diane loved her Uncle Barney. She did not know anything about Dall. Her reality began with Bernard.

29. Hijacking Pies
Chicago Heights, 1955
Richard

Richard was ten years old, very big for his age. He looked twelve. His mother was tall, and he was a throwback to her large German father. His own father had made it back from Japan when he was quite small. Richard did not like his father crawling into mother's bed, not one bit. When she told him it was his Daddy, he had pointed to the photograph of Joseph in his army uniform. Clearly, he wanted Daddy to stay in the picture frame! In due time, of course, the two would become close. Grandma and Grandpa Volcker lived next door. There were a lot of rules in the German households, but most of them made sense to Richard. He still stole pies off Grandma's kitchen window ledge.

Richard loved football and outdoor sports. The entire Uhlaender-Volcker families were athletic. Richard often surprised himself, not realizing his own strength. In future generations, Grandma Uhlaender Volcker's relatives – her nephew Ted Uhlaender and his daughter Katie Uhlaender – would make the family proud. Ted would play major league baseball and Katie would become an Olympian, competing in both Vancouver, Canada, and Sochi, Russia. Oddly, Grandpa Volcker's farm land eventually became the town of Olympia Fields, Illinois. Richard loved his dog, Pepper, with all his heart. Pepper was as important as a human brother or sister to Richard.

30. Eye Problems and James!
Birmingham, England, 1955
Joanne and Alfred, James

Joanne remembered the photographer Alfred - how he had admired her dress and hair. He was quite a bit older, but he treated her like a queen. They married quietly, realizing what they had was unique. Alfred mused about going into insurance. He wanted a family. The entire struggle through the war and afterwards were worth it. He had a prize in Joanne.

Joanne was a brilliant dancer, especially when it came to the jive. Alfred did not mind showing her off. She was young and beautiful. People loved to watch her on the dance floor.

In May 1955, their firstborn arrived. Post-war life was austere in England. Joanne and Alfred lived in a small home on Featherbed Lane. Food was still rationed. Eggs were at a premium. Twenty-one years old, Joanne held James – Jimmy – her newborn son named for his uncle James Hughes.

The first few months were somewhat traumatic. Joanne, who first had eye surgery at age nineteen, lost sight in both eyes six weeks prior to Jimmy's birth. After surgery on her left eye, she had to lie still on her side for three weeks. The doctors feared that childbirth might further harm her eyesight, so she remained in the hospital until after the birth.

When Jimmy was three months old, her right eye required immediate surgery. There was no one to help with Jimmy while Alfred worked and Joanne must again lie still on her side for three weeks. Father Hudson's Home agreed to take James into their nursery so that Joanne could have eye surgery. They commented upon how well the baby had been cared for – so many there had been removed from unfit homes. As Joanne lay recovering, Alfred went to the nursery to see Jimmy. Without notice to Joanne and Alfred, the home had placed him in foster care and the fostering couple thought they were going to adopt James! Albert was in shock and dare not tell Joanne for fear of losing her eyesight entirely. Alfred went into action; he was furious.

Alfred retrieved their baby, but Joanne would be blind in one eye for the rest of her life, as she refused additional corrective surgery on the left eye after the harrowing experience with the nursery. She strengthened herself.

31. Croquet on the Lawn
Davenport, Iowa, 1960
Diane, Harry and Ione, Magna and Bernard

Diane had just turned ten years old when she moved into a new ranch house near a modern elementary school in Iowa. Her dad, Harry had been transferred again. Harry had a knack for taking stores that were running in the red and getting them into the black. A new high school was scheduled to be built very close by. Diane was a bit shy and studious. When she realized that the Iowa kids were ahead of her in math, she was truly afraid. Harry used flash cards to tutor her until she caught up, which took a couple of weeks.

Harry was her whole world, her primary parent by far. She and Ione were not close. Ione had not been able to handle Harry's attention shift after sixteen years of marriage. Diane had flashes of lying in bed ill, waiting for Ione to come check on her, which didn't happen.

Diane sometimes hid in her closet. When Harry came home from work, everything would be okay. Harry's favorite color was yellow, and he was the sunshine in her life. Harry would bring home yellow toilet paper from the store for Ione's pink bathroom. Ione could not train him differently. He liked yellow.

Ione loved her only child, however, and made sure that Diane was the cleanest, best dressed kid around. Ione loved sewing and she made gorgeous outfits for Diane. She would rinse Diane's blonde hair with a special concoction of *Tame* and lemon juice to keep it shiny and blonde. Ione sometimes felt she had given birth, and that was it.

Diane looked and acted like Harry. Ione wished Harry would pay her more attention, his wife. All he thought of was Diane. Ione knew Harry would never forgive her if anything happened to Diane, so she mothered by method of suffocation. Diane seemed to resent it, but Ione did not know what else to do. Ione planted flower seeds in front of the new house. When the flowers came up, they spelled *Diane* in a lovely bed of fuchsia and yellow.

Though Ione had left Illinois, she could still see Illinois across the Mississippi from her new home when she was downtown working. Ione was a fashion plate and went to work as a bridal and better dress consultant. It was very different from the clerical work she was used to, government work. But the schedule was workable and she could buy clothes for her family at a discount. Ione considered food, clothes, and shelter to be the necessities of life. Thus, she justified spending her entire paycheck on clothing, mostly for herself and Diane. Ione often thought about her forty-first birthday dinner, when Diane, but four years old, announced to an entire restaurant that her mother had spent her birthday money on the pretty dress Diane was wearing, then loudly announced Ione's age as well!

Magna and Bernard would sometimes come to Iowa to visit and Diane loved seeing them. Harry and Uncle Barney would let her play croquet with them now, but she never won. Harry and Barney were fun-loving. Ione and Magna, by contrast, always seemed to have the weight of the world on their shoulders, Magna less so.

Magna would often bring a new hankie for Ione's pink satin handkerchief box. Diane loved playing with the box. She could entertain herself for over an hour looking at the hankies, refolding them and putting them back in the box.

Diane's Aunt Magna would tell Diane that the family had come to Illinois because her grandfather disagreed with his brother over the Civil War. Literally, she told Diane, the family split up over the war. Diane was fascinated, as she studied the war in school. Magna and Ione's Grandpa David Birchfield, though originally from Tennessee, eventually moved north to Illinois. Magna told Diane how the Birchfields, Grandma Goldie's family, were prominent in the little town of Erwin, Tennessee, at the base of a mountain. A street there was named for them. Further, Magna told Diane she took Grandma Goldie back to Erwin to visit after World War II. Magna could see Diane was immersed in thoughts about Erwin and the Birchfields – she would tell Diane about Dall Roth another time.

Diane was not close to her Grandma Goldie. They only saw each other on rare occasions. As the last grandchild, Diane was an afterthought, it seemed. Goldie and Ione did not get along, but Goldie gave Ione a piece of pottery from the Pisgah Forest, the work of Walter B. Stephen. Goldie had wanted Ione to marry a rich local farmer. Ione had rebelled, went to college instead and found Harry.

Ione and Harry were married sixteen years when Diane was born. Almost everybody in the family stayed down home, but Ione ran from it. She moved Harry to Chicago in the first place. In Iowa, she was happy they lived close to Illinois, but far enough away from down home.

32. Steaks and Firefighting
Chicago Heights, 1960
Joseph and Lillian, Richard

Richard was fifteen years old and playing football at school. After school, he would help his father at the butcher shop. His mother worked also. He learned to pitch-in for the good of the family. He was large and handsome with gorgeous, clear eyes, and he could lift his much smaller father over his head. Richard was technically minded, and excelled in mathematics, but English and history were a mystery to him.

Richard was an only child, and very close to his parents. Lillian was not able to have more children, so the sun rose and set on Richard. He favored the Volckers, but was also very close to his father. Joseph enjoyed every day with Richard. He considered every day a bonus, courtesy of a bad shot in the Philippines.

Joseph also wanted his son to learn about firefighting. He was a lieutenant in the volunteer fire department, a way to continue doing his duty back at home. He wanted his son to know what it was like to be part of that brotherhood and to help people. He did not want his only child to be terribly spoiled, the Volckers did enough of that! Those pies!

33. *Black is the Color of My True Love's Hair*
Iowa City, Iowa, 1965
Diane, Harry and Ione, Roy and Ardis, Greg, Fred and Willie

Diane sat first chair flute at the University of Iowa summer music camp for junior high youth. She was fifteen. The band consisted of excellent musicians at the junior high level throughout the state of Iowa. She would play a flute solo entitled *Black is the Color of My True Love's Hair*. For decades afterward, the beautiful Scottish ballad would be Diane's warmup song. Her children would be lulled to sleep by it and recognize the melancholy sound in their adult years. But there would be no black-haired man in her life, at least not for a very long time. Diane already had an hourglass figure. She would close her eyes when warming up and imagine how a black-haired love might look. The ballad was a stark contrast to Beatles songs that permeated the nation. Diane loved the Paul McCartney songs, but not so with John Lennon's work.

Harry was of course, very proud of Diane. Ione was too, but she did not show it the way Harry did. She would brag about Diane to others, but never quite mention any of it to Diane.

Harry and Ione were close friends with a couple named Roy and Ardis Wilson who went to the same Methodist church in Davenport. The Wilsons had two sons, both accomplished trombonists. The families were all together for the concert when Diane performed *Black is the Color of My True Love's Hair*. The youngest son, Greg, was Diane's age and like a brother to her. In fact, you might call Greg Harry's son. The two played tennis together and were quite close.

Harry had planned a two-week vacation to Florida following the music camp. He said, "It's high time we visit Fred and Willie in Boca Raton."

Diane and Harry loved the beach experience. Ione tried the seashore, but the first wave knocked her down. She'd had enough and went back to drink coffee with Willie. Harry was just not used to the power of the Florida sun. Both he and Diane were fair haired with Irish skin tone, and both sunburned badly. Harry and Ione spent the next two days sponging Diane's back with vinegar. Harry thought about Hawaii as he dipped the sponge. He also remembered being sunburned with his brothers while swimming at the Sconce Estate pond, the same pond … Dennis …

Harry stopped sponging. Diane asked, "Are you done?"

"No, not quite, Diane," Harry sighed. I was just thinking about when I was a boy. I got sunburned with my brothers. We all had such fair skin because my mother, Alice, was Irish, of course. That's why your skin is so fair. It's really too bad you did not get your mother's skin. She tans so nicely."

Diane thought about Alice for a minute. She had died a few years earlier, but Diane did not really know her. Alice had lost her memory. She thought Harry was somebody else. It frightened Diane to visit Alice.

Finally, Harry finished and Diane realized she hated smelling like vinegar, but she did not complain because the sunburn was more painful than smelling like vinegar. She and her dad rejoined Ione, Fred and Willie in the living room.

Fred was already doing well in real estate. He had built an expensive, custom home with a Grandma Apartment for Willie's mother. He still wanted Harry to join him, but Ione would not hear of it. They had a daughter to finish raising in Iowa. Ione was glued to the Midwest. Besides, she thought, the Florida sun is too hot. Ione did not like the beach.

Harry sighed. He was used to settling for less than what he wanted with Ione. Still, Frank Craig had the prettiest daughters in Champaign County.

34. The Bottling Company
Eau Claire, Wisconsin, 1965
Laverne, Barbara, Janet and her brother Paul

Laverne at his best: running a bottling company and the company was making money. He ran a tight ship. His high-strung ways got things done and done right. Laverne always wore a suit. He popped with ideas. He was a mad man.

He and Barbara had two children, dear Janet and her younger brother Paul. Laverne thought Barbara's relationship with Paul was odd, the way the boy was always attached to her. He constantly found them dancing together and wondered if this was what mental health nurses did. By his fortieth birthday, he gave up. At night, Laverne slept alone in the basement. During the day, he took the world by storm.

Once in a while, Laverne would have a fling with a woman who caught his eye. Emotionally and sexually, Laverne was needy. He never had his fill. This was not the way he wanted life to be, but it was the way his life had evolved. He was warm and geared for passion, passion that never happened with Barbara. But still, he had his duty to his family to think of. There were two children to raise, and he loved them. Janet was the apple of his eye, and she was like Laverne in many ways.

Barbara would visit him in the basement if he invited her. But they always played by her rules. Barbara never really trusted Laverne after the Erika situation, although she never knew there had been a baby. She held back from him to make herself comfortable.

She preferred to study her psychology books and magazines. She wasn't like that "Erika woman," who had just grabbed at a man, that's for sure. Everything was fine, her family perfect. Laverne would settle down and be happy with things the way they were.

35. Tazzing Around
Birmingham, England, 1966
James

James would "taz" around. He was athletic and ran everywhere or used his little bicycle. James was almost too creative. Words, music, lyrics and images all played in his mind constantly. He wore out his mother, Joanne, who had also brought into the world his two younger sisters, June and Annie. He wanted his mother to like the words he wrote and the things he did. Sometimes his Uncle Jim would show him how to play the harmonica and Auntie Olga showed him a bit about the piano, but James was fascinated by the guitar.

James did well in school and did not realize how well comparatively. He was almost too sensitive for the soccer field, but he loved it. He was already part of youth soccer and loved to go with his father, Alfred, to see Birmingham City Football Club, *The Blues*, play at St. Andrew's ground (stadium). They would park the car down the hill and walk uphill to the ground then stand and watch the game. The air was electric at the games. James loved going to St. Andrew's.

Joanne and Alfred took the kids camping in Bristol. The entire family loved nature and the outdoors. They were able to watch the World Cup on a television in the office area there. England won!

36. Winning
Virginia Beach, Virginia, 1968
Harry and Ione, Diane and Steve

Harry's chest puffed out with pride as he hurried back to celebrate at the hotel in Virginia Beach. He and Ione were in charge of the band parents' organization. Harry had personally raised enough money to send ten kids to Virginia Beach, including Diane, of course, who sat first chair flute. Harry made sure Diane's friend Elizabeth, who played the oboe, could make the trip. Her dad was an injured veteran.[5] Harry had a real soft spot for Elizabeth's dad. The band had just won the entire competition – concert, marching, and sight reading – top in all categories. It had been dramatic. After a two-hour concert by the Navy Band, a huge banner was unfurled with their school's name on it. Harry carried a large slate of blue ribbons back to the hotel, one for each band member. He was happy it had been the Navy Band.

Diane was ecstatic the competition was over and they had won, but her mind was on her upcoming wedding. Steve had chased her, insistent in the beginning, taking her away from her boyfriend Bill,

---

[5] Art Goodman was not allowed to reveal his locations during WWII, so his family is still tracking where he was when he "mostly lost his feet". Somewhere north of Paris, they believe. His brother, Bob, still living in 2014, tells of that day. Art had been Captain of an ordnance disposal unit and, as such, had been destroying bombs and capturing ordnance usable by the Allies in the Les Haies [The Hedges] area, at the border of France and Belgium. The extensive farm, just northeast of Paris, was land owned by a Belgian family once devoted to the Rothschild family wineries in the 19th Century. On June 19, 1945, as part of a mop up operation, Art was still "somewhere north of Paris". He tripped on a British grenade and his feet were mostly blown away from his body. Art had been leading a unit of his own men and German prisoners. It had been necessary to draw a gun on the Germans to procure enough help for his own men. The Germans wanted to leave Art for dead. His friend, Bob Morris, helped him that day, while Art tied up his own feet using his belt as a tourniquet. Art was born in 1921, in Minneapolis, near Robert Vaughan, who, in 1969, would star in *The Bridge at Remagen*, the movie.

but she loved his positive ways and all the laughter he provided. Steve was athletic and strong, although he had grown several inches in height. At age eighteen, he contracted meningitis. He had almost died then, but now was the picture of health. They were scheduled to wed and set out for Iowa City, where he would be a junior and she would start college. The War raged in Vietnam. Steve had a student deferment. Harry seemed to have already made Steve his son-in-law, but Ione didn't like men much, including Steve. Steve was from a farm, and Ione hated that fact. Ione was, however, looking forward to having Harry back.

A tickertape parade awaited the band as their three busses rolled over the Mississippi River bridge. Diane was chosen to be in the convertible leading the parade and waving at everybody. Her blonde hair blew in the warm summer breeze; she had fun.

37. Finding the Right Niche
South of Chicago, 1968
Lillian and Joseph, Richard and Mary

Lillian had introduced Richard to Mary after he returned from Purdue having not done well there. He had warmed the bench for the Purdue football team, and his studies had not been much better. He was just not cut out for all that English and history. Richard was a technical person; he had been bent on getting an education in the budding computer industry, but Joseph thought he was nuts. Joseph didn't see computers going anywhere. Still, Richard loved the field. He enrolled in a local technical college and did well. By the fall of 1968, he was very gainfully employed, married to Mary, his mother's choice, and had two children, born close together. He was on top of the world, but could not always control his temper. Joseph's tendencies had rubbed off.

Joseph was a meat cutter, a damn good meat cutter. A real butcher. He rivaled his wife at cooking as well. Joseph had made his only son Richard work when he was quite young, and the young man knew how to butcher meat correctly. Joseph still considered every day a bonus, every day since the bullet zinged past his head in the Philippines. Lillian, being quite technical herself, worked for the telephone company, *Ma Bell*. She was proud of her young sister, Bethany, who was already in California working for the government in a very technical capacity. Bethany would wind up at the Jet Propulsion Laboratory in Pasadena, California.

38. Sal! + Shock and Despair
Iowa City, 1970
Steve and Diane, Ione

Steve had not been doing well in a math class the semester Sal was born. His math instructor was Chinese and Steve could not understand a word the man said. He dropped the class, not realizing he would become a part-time student. Steve was all for a lesser load as he worked nights at a local factory to support Diane and Sal. Sal had been born in September of 1969. It was clear they were a very fertile couple.

"This baby has red hair!" Ione stated, holding the little girl up to the sunlight.

"No!" said Diane. "She is blonde, like me."

Ione scowled. The baby had red hair. Ione was right. Red hair and green eyes, just like Harry's Irish mother, Alice. Ione wondered if any of her characteristics would ever show up anywhere!

Then everything went haywire. As a part-time student, Steve lost his draft deferment. Unable to take a family deferment after claiming fulltime student status, he had his pre-induction physical and passed with flying colors.

Diane was stunned because of these circumstances. In less than two years, she had gone from waving on a convertible to holding her red-headed daughter in her arms and thinking about her husband going to Vietnam. She was unprepared emotionally for any of this and Steve was just talking about doing his duty. Very soon, the county-by-county lottery went into effect. Steve drew number 123. They would not know until the end of the year whether Scott County, Iowa, would draft soldiers up to that number or not. He had a reprieve, but still, they were on tenterhooks.

The fall semester started with their home county not yet reaching Steve's number. By November, Diane and Steve were starting to hope they might make it. Things were looking up. Diane had invited her friend, Sue, up for the weekend from home; she was going out on a date with Steve's friend and they had all enjoyed a few beers. It was quite late when the phone rang, past midnight, but they were all sitting in the living room, or what you would call a living room in a WWII Quonset hut home.

Diane answered the phone. The voice on the other end was strained. It was one of her parents' friends. She wanted to put Ione on the phone to speak to Diane. Diane's own heart froze solid as she heard Ione say the words that Harry had suffered a heart attack on the dance floor. He was dead. Diane's Daddy was dead. She dropped the phone. All was a blur. She saw Steve run for the dangling phone as she fell to the floor. It seemed like hours went by before the first seared sob came out of her. The entire world spun in an unreal vortex of pain. Never had a daughter loved a father more than Diane loved Harry. Nothing would ever be the same. For Diane, age twenty, losing her father would remain the worst event ever for decades to come.

Steve and Sue tried to console her all the way to the river, some fifty miles, but Diane remained silent, unable to think or talk. Steve's optimism, for once, rang hollow. They dropped off Sal with Steve's parents.

The next morning the Wilsons were there, along with her proxy-brother Greg. Greg looked almost as lost as Diane. He had just been with Harry the day before. In future years, Greg and Diane would be at the funerals of all four parents. They would not let each other down. But Harry's was the first. Diane was in shock and could not function.

At one point, Steve's parents brought over Sal. She was almost fifteen months old and running around. The toddler went from room to room, looking for her best buddy, Grandpa Harry. She could not find him, and Diane's heart broke even further. Sal was a sweetie with red hair and green eyes, just like Harry's Irish mother. Ione had previously complained that Harry monopolized Sal; now Diane was glad he had done so. In future years, Diane would think how wonderful it was that Harry died on the dance floor. But for now, her mind and heart were too ice-filled to think any such thought. She stared at Sal's red hair and thought about how Harry's beard was red if it started to grow out. Red hair, like Alice.

20. Harry and Ione (holding Sal) at campus shortly before Harry's untimely death.

Harry was with Alice now. He had crossed over in the fall of his fifty-eighth year.

Diane's only solace was the arrival of her Aunt Magna and Uncle Bernard. Diane was twenty years old, and Magna thought it was time she knew about her Uncle Dall. Magna explained that Harry and Dall were best friends married to sisters. She told Diane he died in the war, but no particulars. In future years, when Diane would ask, Ione would tell her that Dall died in the Battle of the Bulge.

Uncle Barney stood next to Harry's casket and read Harry's favorite, the Twenty-third Psalm. Diane could not handle it; she collapsed. The only memory she would have of Steve during this time would be that he asked her to make him a sandwich; she did not remember any comfort coming from him. He, too, was young and unprepared for this.

Vernon Williams stood looking at the body of his Uncle Harry. He had buried his own father, Harry's older brother Irvin, only the year before. He smiled and thought about a young lad sprung off a boat at Pearl Harbor. God, that island had been gorgeous. "Thank-you, Harry," he whispered over the casket.

Sheryl Williams Sypult, Don's only child, had buried Don the year before Uncle Irvin. All three brothers had suffered heart attacks. Sheryl was almost in the same state as Diane, green eyes brimming with tears for hours on end.

39. Jacob!
Iowa City and Wisconsin, 1972
Diane and Steve, Sal and Jacob, Ione

Pregnant again and fairly blissful, Diane read and studied Harry's writings after he died. She discovered her spiritual self. After Harry died, yellow roses would spring up at unusual times and always seem to indicate his presence. His singing would ring in her head. "But the yellow rose of Texas is the only girl for me!" Diane would cry over those lyrics.

Diane was in her seventh month, and it was difficult to hold Sal centered on her lap; Sal loved to read books together. Sal was almost three, so Diane had her sit to the side in the big gold chair they used for reading. Sal felt a little put out by this, but after all, Diane was still reading to her.

It was time for the move to Wisconsin. Steve had completed his master's degree in earth science teaching and had garnered one of the few teaching jobs available, mainly due to the fact that he had built a planetarium and earned a master's degree. Diane had typed his master's thesis while he worked and she very pregnant - page by page on an old typewriter; errors and corrections not allowed. Diane thought it didn't hurt that she sat in on Steve's job interview as a pregnant wife. He was to teach at a brand new junior high school in Wisconsin and a little house had been rented. Diane loved the fireplace there, with built-ins on each side. The left side built-in was a drop down desk with cubby holes for keeping track of the bills, and the right side was a mullioned glass door cabinet where she could put books. Sal loved books, Diane realized acutely.

The move was accomplished and Diane made short order of the Wisconsin driving test. Once the patrolman saw how advanced her pregnancy was, the test became very short indeed! The school year started, relatives came for Sal's third birthday, and Diane awaited the birth of their next child. Diane wanted two children, but no more. She could not imagine herself as the original earth mother. Two children would be plenty. Diane was somewhat liberal with sympathies towards the women's movement. Steve did not like that! But, being an earth scientist, he did agree with "zero population growth".

Steve got the son he wanted, and Diane was also ecstatic to have a girl and a boy. Jacob, however, did not enter the world healthy. Diane was Rh negative, but both her children were Rh positive. Despite treatment after Sal's birth, baby Jacob experienced jaundice due to a high bilirubin count. There was talk of blood transfusions for Jacob and questions about whether he would go home with his Mom.

Ione rode a bus to Wisconsin as soon as she got word that her

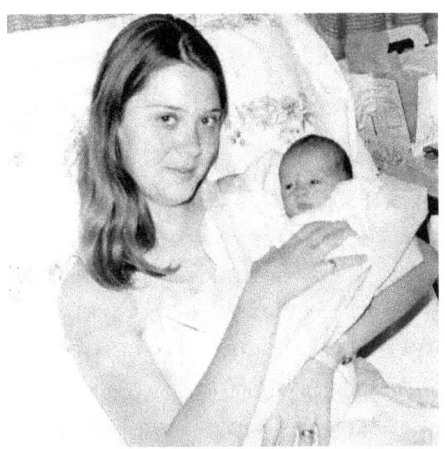

21. Diane and Jacob, 1972.

grandson had been born. When Steve brought her to the hospital, baby Jacob, almost seven pounds, lay naked under a light with his eyes patched. He suffered jaundice. Unfortunately, nurses placed a bruising nine-pound baby nearby, and Ione panicked.

"What's wrong with our baby?" she cried.

The nurses explained, but Ione barely heard. She was not over Harry's death, not in the least. Jacob responded to treatment and went home with his Mom after all. Sal was waiting in the car with Grandma; her green eyes became as big as saucers. From that day forward, Jacob was her baby. Diane had been terribly worried about Jacob, in reality. No more babies, she thought. She would be pressing her luck.

Ione stayed two weeks, then went home to Iowa. She had planned a trip to Hawaii, as she had never seen it with Harry. She would go with a group.

40. Long, Wavy Black Hair
December, 1972; England
James, Joanne and Alfred

James was seventeen years old and very ill. His stomach was in knots; the initial doctor had diagnosed gastric problems. The following morning, Joanne found James rolling on his bed screaming and holding his head. Alfred brought the car around and they headed for the hospital. Alfred ran in and brought out some of the staff; they put James into a wheelchair immediately and brought him in.

Underneath his long, shoulder-length, excessively wavy black hair, James was having a brain hemorrhage and his life was in danger, but that was not yet known. Tests began. Joanne was alone, as Alfred, out of real necessity, had to keep working. James was in a terrible state. He could not talk or move his hands. Joanne was taken for a private consultation and it was explained that his only hope would be at Smethwick Hospital.

Alfred had arranged to meet Joanne in the car park. As soon as she was in the car, she was so upset she could not speak and burst out crying. Alfred thought the boy was dead.

"No, no," Joanne gasped. "He is just so very ill and I don't know what is happening."

They went back into the hospital to find James sedated. He was sitting up now and feeling better. He began making slurred jokes with Joanne and Alfred; none of which they appreciated from their teenaged son. Known to be a character, he had allowed himself to be suspended from school one day over his hair. He would stand at the blackboard and mimic the master before they would enter the room; of course, he sometimes got caught.

"I suppose this will be the death of me," he said, giddy with drugs. His parents failed to see the *humour*.

Early next morning, James woke to the sound of motorcycles and radios. The nurse explained that was his ride to the Midland Centre for Neurosurgery and Neurology at Smethwick. They had an escort of eight police motorcycle outriders. Sitting up straight, James thought it great fun to speed from the south to north side of Brum like a hot knife through butter. They had taken him before Joanne and Alfred could even get to the hospital.

The Smethwick hospital was one of the leaders in neurology in Europe and James was one of the first to experience an NMR, the forerunner of the MRI. It was thought he might have a tumor. Additionally, two holes were drilled in his head and air pumped in. James had the longest hair in school, but now it had to be shaved. At age seventeen, he was not happy about that and now was more focused on his hair. In reality, he had a cerebral hemorrhage. A blood clot the size of a large walnut had formed and lodged itself between the brain and cerebellum. This had formed from an aneurysm at the top of his head, caused by a broken nose obtained on the soccer pitch at St. Andrew's. At the time, considering his age, James thought it wonderful to be on the same treatment table in the St. Andrew's locker room as Bob Latchford and Trevor Francis, his soccer heroes.

The operation was on Joanne's birthday, the 8th of December. She was thirty-eight years old and this was a rough one, but she would make it through. Her son, she felt, must make it through. The clot was removed. Before the surgery, James just knew he was going to die. He felt like he was just waiting for a bus and would see what came next; he actually felt calm. He was wrong; he survived. The surgeon, Mr. Hamilton, had done brilliant work. Six days after the surgery, James persuaded the nurses to let him out of bed. The nurses balked, but James was insistent. Reluctantly, they helped him, as he was hell-bent to do it. Once up, he walked relatively normally, and the nurses all wept. He went home on Boxing Day, and was back in school a few weeks later, without his long wavy black hair.

James was back in rehearsals for *The Sorcerer* by Gilbert and Sullivan in no time at all.

The teenagers formed letters on stage. James slanted into the shape of an N. Then all collapsed on stage as part of the scene. When everybody got up, James did not. He was unconscious and soon back in the hospital. In the end, it was only a slight set back; he was back in school and on his way to college in no time. He was about to turn eighteen.

James had to take his A-Levels right after brain surgery, so he did not do as well on the exams as had been expected. He did pass the Oxford entrance exam, but studying at Oxford was unaffordable. He was then directed to a local art college, where he studied what he loved: painting, theater, teaching. After what seemed like indulgence to him, there was a living to be made. James procured a white collar job in the steelworks at Corby at the age of twenty-one. Commerce would become his game.

41. New Houses

Wisconsin 1975, Iowa 1975
Ione and John T., Diane and Steve, Frank Craig's portrait, Magna and Bernard

In Wisconsin: Ione was to remarry. She had gone dancing and found a nice gentleman, a widower ten years her senior. She did not want a divorced man. John T. had run the Iowa branch of John Hancock Insurance. He was a member of the country club. An avid golfer, John had made a hole-in-one earlier in life. He had played minor league baseball. He was a gentleman and fairly formal.

Ione had decided to help Diane and Steve procure a home in Wisconsin, as they were struggling on one starting teacher's salary. She gave them a down payment and Diane started looking.

In the end, they bought a house right around the corner from their rental. Diane loved the large and spacious three-bedroom home. The basement was finished with paneling and carpeting, and there was a play room off the kitchen for the kids that had windows all around dark pine v-groove paneling.

Ione had long ago given Diane the portrait of Frank Craig - anything to get it out of her house. Diane loved the gorgeous dark walnut oval frame and convex glass. She hung Grandpa Frank in the dining room. He had long been dead by the time Diane was born.

Diane had never been happier. She and Steve wallpapered the first floor bedroom for Jacob – all the walls were covered with traffic signs of all kinds – the room was light and airy. The largest bedroom upstairs was given over to Sal – she had so many things. She had wooden doll beds, and Steve's sister and brother-in-law had made her the cutest wooden kitchen set – three pieces painted avocado green. A plastic bowl had been inserted as the sink, and dishwasher soap bottles could be filled from underneath – the spouts acted as faucets.

Sal had to share her closet with her mother, but that was okay. She had a lovely dormer window and put the doll beds there. Sal was the keeper of all the books also; she was already reading to her younger brother. Her Grandma Ione joined book clubs and the books arrived in the mail.

Diane painted small bookcases avocado green with a black glaze and put them in Sal's room.

Ione was moving into John T.'s furnished home, so she gave Diane and Steve the lion's share of her furniture. A house full of furniture helped Diane to feel even more happy and stable. Ione was closing a chapter as best she could and helping Diane and her young family. She felt good about that.

Diane had discovered her spiritual self when Harry died, and she wanted the kids in Sunday school, so they joined the local Methodist church. Jacob's Sunday school teacher was a woman named Janet; she fell in love with the young Jacob's sparkling aqua-hazel eyes and brown, tightly-curled hair. Ione's coloring had finally made an appearance in little Jacob. His dark curls were so tight they would "boing" if you pulled on them. Janet thought he was a very special little boy. Diane and Janet became fast friends.

In Iowa: Ione's wedding was lovely. Ione bought new clothes for Sal and Jacob, and of course, a dress for Diane to attend her. John T. was Catholic, but they did allow Ione's Methodist pastor to take part. The Saucony suit Ione had bought for Jacob was precious, a one-piece short navy blue set and he wore long stockings to the knees. The only problem was that three-year-old Jacob made it known he hated the suit! Decades later he would remember how much he hated that suit. Jacob pouted all day, but Sal was fine with her green dress, setting off her green eyes.

Magna and Bernard were there. Diane was twenty-five years old and was becoming aware of how much Magna and Ione had experienced together. The dinner was held at Jumer's Castle Lodge. Diane sat next to her favorite Aunt and asked more questions. "What year did Dall die? When did Aunt Magna marry Uncle Barney?"

"1945 and 1949," Magna answered.

Diane replied, "You started a whole new life right before I was born, didn't you Magna?"

"Yes, dear, just in time to run to the hospital the night you almost died."

"I'm sorry I did that to you, Aunt Magna!" Diane exclaimed.

"It's all right dear, you are here and your Mom needs you now. You are so much like Harry."

Indeed, Ione would put Diane right in Harry's place, with the same expectations of self-sacrifice. Harry and Diane had learned self-neglect, for Ione was always "sick". In later years, Diane would realize that her mother and aunts only had attention out on the farm from their own mother if they were sick. Grandma Goldie had not been nurturing. She fought constantly with her sisters and fought with her husband over sex.

Diane thought to herself. Indeed, she was like Harry. Diane looked at the yellow roses decorating the table and thought about that crazy song that Harry used to sing: "The Yellow rose of Texas is the only girl for me!"

42. Janet and Kitchens
Eau Claire, 1977
Diane and Janet, Laverne

Diane had wanted to study architecture or journalism in college. Music had not appealed to her, and she did not want to teach band. Old-school-Harry, born in 1912, forbade both architecture and journalism. Neither were for women, he flatly stated. He wanted Diane to teach, but she had not finished her teaching degree. Finances and babies were prohibitive, but also Diane just did not want to be a teacher. Or a nurse, Harry's other suggestion. She had walked away from college with a near four-point grade average, completely disillusioned, after a couple of years. After Harry died, Ione had refused to give Diane her paid up insurance policy or pay for college from Harry's life insurance, so Diane put her education on the back burner. But after four plus years in Wisconsin, she was a bit bored. Jacob was past four years old and she wanted to be part of the adult world again; he was old enough for a pre-school.

Diane had occupied her time at home drawing house plans for fun with no formal training. It was just what she did. One day, she confided in Janet that she would like to work or go back to school, but lacked direction.

Janet was pregnant and lit up like a Christmas tree. "You could replace me at my dad's showroom. I will teach you what to do. We have not known what we were going to do with my baby coming. It's sooo difficult to find people who can live up to my dad's expectations, but I know you can do it. We design and sell kitchens."

Diane did not know what that involved. She thought the builders just sort of did the kitchens. Diane spoke with her best friend, Lea, who had four children at the time. They often drank coffee together, discussing God, politics, and childrearing. This time Diane was expressing to Lea that she just needed to be out in the adult world. Lea always had the wisdom of the world in her eyes. She was not sure Diane was doing the right thing, and besides, she hated to lose her coffee buddy.

Diane decided to ask Janet more about the job. "Is it just tracking inventory and delivering to builders?"

"Oh no," Janet replied. "It is more complex than that. But I know you like to draw plans for fun. It will be easy for you." My dad is a bit *Army*, but you can handle him, I think." Janet explained, "He is a decorated war hero. Europe, you know. He likes everything to be shipshape. If you can start working there, I could stay home and draw plans from there after the baby comes."

With all work arrangements made, Jacob entered the Jack and Jill preschool. Sal was already in the second grade and quite the independent young lady. On her first day of kindergarten, and not yet five years old, Sal insisted that Diane not accompany her. Diane followed her to school, Jacob in tow, hiding behind trees. All the other kids were crying and hanging onto their mothers - but not Sal. She thought kindergarten was the bee's knees, and wondered what could be wrong with the other kids.

43. Square Dancing
Chicago Heights, 1978
Richard

Richard, the main-stay of his family, ran the show. He was dominant and commanded the kids, took care of the house and kept Mary secure. Mary did not work outside the home, contending as best she could with her children. Richard had built a second story on the house. He and Joseph had completely retiled the lower level bathroom themselves. He lowered the ceilings to help save heating costs and did everything himself. He was highly independent and loved being a family man. He had done well in the corporate world and had survived a couple of takeovers. His skills with computer hardware were being honed.

When he wasn't busy with his job and the house, he and Mary would square dance in western gear. He loved it. Always the biggest man in the square, his grip was so severe that he caught people off guard. A volunteer firefighter, no matter what he was doing, if the fire bell rang, away he would go. At one point, he found out what it was like to carry someone out of a burning building; it felt good. Richard was the biggest dog lover that his family had ever been aware of. To him, dogs were people.

44. Kitchens and More
Eau Claire, 1979
Diane, Laverne

Diane turned out to be a natural kitchen designer, a creative space planner. The training came to her easily. The bookkeeping side was a snap. She had Harry's mind for mathematics and business. She thought of Harry. If only he were not dead when she needed him most. She had walked to work in the morning from the East Side Hill, along the river by the Uniroyal rubber plant, but it still had not been enough time to pull herself together.

She fought back tears that pushed at her eyeballs. Her boss was ex-military, a member of the *Lightning Division* in WWII, and his license plate proudly displayed the emblem. He tolerated no nonsense. Yet, she had to admit, his attitude had softened over the two years she worked for him. Janet's dad Laverne had a soft side, decorated war hero or not. In fact – no, she was probably wrong about there being something else – something more than a soft side.

The tears pushed past insistently. "Good God! What's wrong with you, Diane?" Laverne had seen her. She swirled her stool away from him, but he circled the counter. He would be furious at this happening in his showroom, simply furious.

"I'm so sorry, Laverne," she whispered. More tears. "I'm having trouble at home … just give me a minute."

"Diane," he said almost sweetly, "go back to my office please."

"Oh God," she thought, "I don't need any army reprimand or pep talk."

She sat across from him in the same chair used to give out her daily assignments. "What's going on here, Diane?" he queried. There was an odd look on his face. She might as well tell him; things might not get better soon.

"Marital problems," she said.

"You had an argument?"

"No argument," she sighed. "It's worse than that."

"Are you sure, Diane?"

"Yes. Medical evidence", she whispered.

The room went so silent. Diane supposed giving marriage advice might not be Laverne's strong point. Would he tell Janet? God, it could be all over the church. "I would appreciate it if you didn't mention this to Janet," Diane said, looking sideways at the cabinet delivery schedule on the wall.

"I don't have Janet on my mind just now, Diane," he said softly. Something in his voice turned Diane's head toward his. There it was. That other thing about him she had not been able to identify. Laverne removed his black glasses.

"Do you know what FUBAR means, Diane?"

She shook her head. No.

"It means, Fucked-Up-Beyond-All-Recognition. And that's what your husband must be. I've been in love with you for over a year, Diane. Please understand I am not trying to harass you or take advantage of you while you are this upset. I am simply telling you the truth. The war is over. It's not an ideal world. These are the facts, Diane. I know there is a hell of an age difference here and you probably think I am nuts."

The room went silent again. Diane knew there was attraction between them. She just had not admitted it. He was her boss and Janet's dad. And he too was married. "Jesus," she thought, "I need help."

"Do you love your husband, Diane?" asked Laverne.

Why was that such a tough question? Earlier this year had been their eleventh anniversary. They had gone dancing and danced to *Do That to Me One More Time* by the Captain and Tennille. It had been good, romantic and emotional. In years to come, Diane would realize Steve had already been involved with Katherine before the anniversary dance. "I guess so," she answered weakly. "You just go on day to day, don't you? I love my children and my house and our life so much."

Laverne pressed her. "Do you love your life or your husband, or both?"

Why did it seem so clear and simple for Laverne? Surely he knew what she meant. He had been married to his high school sweetheart, raised a family, went to church and work. Surely he could see the complications.

Silence filled the room. Laverne's coffee, always with cream, had grown cold. "I don't know," she said. "I need to dry my eyes and go back to work and think."

"All right," he responded. "You aren't going to quit your job now, are you, Diane?"

"No," she said, I love my job."

Laverne wondered if he had a chance. She was twenty-seven years his junior. "Christ," he murmured aloud, "she wasn't even born yet when I left Germany and the bridge behind me." He opened his desk and looked at the Bronze Star. He thought about his buddy Dall. Dall always said his wife Magna and her sisters were the prettiest women in Champaign County. Frank Craig's girls, he called them. Well, Diane had to be the prettiest in this county - at least in his eyes. He wondered if she was as passionate under all that efficiency as he was. He thought about Erika.

***

Weeks later, trembling in his arms, Laverne had his answer. She had to be sure he wasn't just a port in the storm, she had said. She had to be sure he was not a father figure. Laverne wasn't sure why that was so important. He knew Diane's father was dead and gone and her mother remarried in another state.

22. Laverne's Bronze Star.

Laverne sat on a hotel room chair smoking. His suit was neatly placed over the other chair; nothing was ever sloppy with Laverne. He was experienced with women, but this was different. He was more in love than he knew he could be and was incapable of thinking beyond that moment. This was the love he left Germany behind to find, the one that made it all worthwhile.

He was done with his smoke. She was relaxed in the bed and her eyes were closed, but she spoke. "I've never been as happy as in this moment, aside from motherhood."

"Thank God," thought Laverne as he wisely left the smokes behind and went back to her. His favorite song, *For the Good Times*, played in his head.

45. Stark Reality
England, 1980
James

James thought to himself, it must be just luck if a guy picks the right girl. On his own in Corby, he had married a pretty young thing who had three children. Something inside James always drove him to a family situation. Besides, she was sexy. He was naive and drawn in by her. In reality, she was an alcoholic. Their own son, born with fetal alcohol syndrome in 1979, would grow up disabled in various ways.

James was drowning in his emotions and panic, but he would do his duty to his family. He would work hard and somehow try to hold it all together. When she was drunk, there would be nasty fights. She had thrown bottles at him and had even injured him. His entire family disliked his wife intensely.

Career wise James did well. The steelworks had put him into executive training. He liked the public relations field. Music often soothed his soul. A little Paul Simon or Deep Purple suited him.

46. Alive and Well
Eau Claire, 1980
Diane, Laverne, Steve

Diane had never felt so alive. Laverne brought out the entire woman in her, the businesswoman and the basic woman. Suddenly aware of her talent, she realized a finer level of nuance in her work. Her creativity rose and her entire being burst with love.

Laverne explained the Federal Reserve Bank, bless him. Steve was too busy with his own concerns to notice. Increasingly MIA from home on general principle, he was either working a second job, playing any one of the six sports he was involved with, slow and fast-pitch softball, basketball, skiing, weightlifting, motocross and golf. Diane had no idea what he did with the money from his second job; it never went into the household or created family benefits in any way that she could see. Diane saw Laverne when she could. Of course they worked together every day, but she spent most of her free time with her children. She pushed Steve's increasing absences to the back of her mind and pushed on with life.

Diane now lived between her kids and the office and Laverne. Laverne bought her an egg salad sandwich every Friday and they would share lunch on that day. Normally, Laverne went home for lunch, as he preferred a short noontime nap in his basement retreat. Diane usually did her bookwork while he was gone, unless a customer came in unexpectedly; most clients came in by appointment. Sometimes the outside salesman came in to cover late in the afternoon. They would say Diane had to leave to get kids at school. Laverne would say he had an appointment, but of course they would be down the street at the hotel. Or sometimes they would meet there on Saturday if time allowed. There wasn't really time for many hotel meetings, so Diane treasured each one. Every encounter was more intense than the one before, more emotional. It seemed as if they knew there would not be a permanent solution to their love affair.

Then there had been the time they went to Minneapolis for the day to a supposed kitchen exposition. They walked arm in arm and some people did notice the age difference, but it was a more metropolitan environment certainly than the home town. After an exotic Chinese lunch, they checked into a luxury hotel. Just once, he wanted to live it up a bit with her. Laverne liked things to be first class; he drove the Lincoln town car with the *Lightning* license plates.

Laverne studied her over lunch. He really wasn't that hungry, except for her once again. He had ceased trying to figure out the chemistry he felt with Diane. He'd experienced nothing like it before. Maybe with Erika, although he had always thought that to be war release. Certainly, he was a fumbling lover with Erika compared to Diane. Diane told him she had only been with her husband and him, no others. She had married young. She belonged in this luxury environment, he thought.

Diane was saying something about the restaurant lighting when he tuned back in for a minute. Laverne watched as she turned and pointed, sweater tightening against her D-sized breasts.

"It's gorgeous," he said. "Let's go to the room now."

47. Anger
Chicago Heights, 1980
Richard, Mary

Richard and Mary had loud, wild fights. Richard's temper often got the best of him. The kids followed suit. They never got along as brother and sister. Sometimes they would call Joseph and Lillian and bring them into it. The whole family was out of control. Joseph had quite a temper himself. He was known to bully people. But he and Lillian did not fight like Richard and Mary. Richard and Mary were really something.

Richard's daughter, his eldest child, came home drunk once. She would eventually earn advanced degrees, but that day she was stone-cold drunk. The kid who got her drunk showed up the next morning and Richard had made it out to the front sidewalk on one leap and taught that kid a thing or two. Richard was a huge man who would intimidate anyone.

Richard's son also became loud and given to anger, although both were known for joking and humor as well. Richard worked too hard; that was part of his problem. At his core, he was a good man, a good man who did not know how to cope with certain things. His son looked up to him.

48. Leaving for Chicago
Eau Claire, 1981
Laverne and Diane, Sal

Laverne gave Diane a sparkling necklace with two gold hearts entwined. It was how he felt, and she had to know. She was leaving now; she was moving to Chicago. She could not marry him and cause another family's destruction. She could not see him raising kids again. She just could not do it. She was hoping her talent would forge a dynamic career in the Chicago market.

Diane's husband finally came clean, admitting he wanted to marry his school secretary at all cost. There was the usual distress. Diane and Steve decided upon joint custody, or rather, Steve dictated joint custody. Sal would go to Chicago with Diane. Jacob would spend the school year with his father.

Diane went along with whatever Steve said, frankly. She didn't have the money for a lawyer. The loss of her home and family unit left her in shock. Her brain felt frozen. She did believe Steve when he told her the junior high boys he taught who were in trouble were all being raised by single mothers. Steve had been the disciplinarian. Diane, like her father Harry before her, was way too soft-hearted towards her children. They were good kids. She didn't think they needed browbeating. It was best Steve would deal with a teenaged son, no doubt, but Jacob was only nine and Diane's heart was breaking. She did trust Steve where Jacob was concerned, and that was, "Worth its weight in gold," as Harry used say. But Harry was not there to help Diane.

Diane had arranged a job in Chicago, and now it was time to go. Initially, Steve had planned to stick her in a firetrap apartment near the kids' school so he could afford the divorce. He was fairly shocked himself at her leaving Wisconsin, but he had prepared the divorce for a while, planned it with Katherine.

He informed Diane she could not take his son away and if she tried to get full custody, she could not leave Wisconsin. With no money or job, Diane felt she was now trapped into taking the job in

Chicago to make a living; either that or she and Sal would be starving somewhere in Wisconsin. She would always feel that things went Steve's way under threat.

Later, Diane would still be in shock at her losses when the judge asked her if she was okay with the divorce settlement, and she replied, "Yes."

Decades later when picking up paperwork for another purpose, a county clerk would say to her, "Oh my, there is a sealed letter from the judge in your divorce file."

Indeed. "Well," thought Diane, "I suppose the judge didn't think it very fair and left me a way to object." At the time she was hell-bent to do it all on her own. She identified when the singing-star Cher said, "You take his money, and you take his shit." The letter remained in the file. Unopened.

Due to the joint custody, Diane received no financial support from Steve other than a token amount because he claimed the children on his income tax. She also had no alimony. Diane gave the income tax return directly to Sal, and Sal handled her own budget for incidentals.

Diane's new job paid her on commission, so it would take a while to build up income. Her mother, Ione, refused to help with even one penny from Harry's insurance money. She said it was, "Steve's problem." In the end, Laverne supported Diane and Sal for the first three months, but of course nobody knew that was the case.

Initially, Diane went to Chicago to arrange for the move. Sal did not handle her mother's absence well. Making matters worse, on Thanksgiving Day, with Diane in Chicago, Steve invited Katherine to have dinner with the children. Diane thought Steve was an idiot, and became angry with him. Katherine never quite left and Diane stayed angry for some time afterward. She would never get over the feeling that she'd been ambushed. Everything happened too quickly and was too planned by others, probably because Katherine's husband had invited her to leave. Diane and Steve never even discussed their marriage.

"Well," thought Diane, "maybe there was nothing left to discuss." She hated talking to him anyway. He was down-your-throat, "my way or the highway," though he usually did it with a grin on his face. He was never, ever violent. Diane mused, "Guess it is the highway." She would miss her friend, Lea, but hoped to see her in Chicago, as it was Lea's home city. Janet was busy with two children now. Diane hoped she could ease out of that relationship since Janet was Laverne's daughter. Leaving gave her an excuse to do so.

The transition from Eau Claire to Chicago was a day-to-day, nightmarish struggle for Diane. Clearly, she was in shock. She could not stay in Eau Claire and watch Steve and Katherine happy while denying her own life with Laverne. Laverne managed the business for a remote owner, and he did not have the authority to pay Diane five times more than what she was making, but that kind of increase is what she would need to be the primary bread winner for a household. Diane knew she had the talent to make a dent in the Chicago market – she had her eye on the far west suburbs of Wheaton and Glen Ellyn. There she could find excellent schools for Sal. Diane felt she had two choices – give in to Laverne's desire for marriage and hurt more people, or forge her own better living in a primary market.

In addition, from Chicago's west suburbs, it was just a hop over Illinois Hwy-5 to Diane's hometown of Davenport, Iowa. Ione had been out in Iowa over twenty years now. She and her husband were ailing and in need of support. Diane's stepsister, Joan, was a teacher in Chicago's northwest suburbs and looked forward to seeing Diane's children more often. Together, they hoped to manage whatever came up with Ione and John T. out in Iowa. In addition, Sue was nearby, in Batavia. As an only child, Diane felt she needed whatever support she could garnish.

The fall of 1981 felt like a thunderbolt striking Diane's soul. One minute she had been planting daffodil bulbs around the front lamp-post of the home she loved. Then the thunderbolt. Everything was turned upside-down. Diane would not be in the house the following spring when the yellow daffodils pushed through the earth. There would be no yellow flowers for Diane, no songs by Harry. Laverne looked so forlorn the last time she walked out of his showroom. The heartbreak showed heavily on his face.

"Please Laverne," she said, "please do right by your family. They are important." Diane could barely walk to her car. Steve had never looked at her with such love in their entire marriage.

Still, Steve was shook up. He had not planned on anybody leaving his immediate control. He cried over Sal leaving. He wound up taking so much aspirin that his stomach ulcerated. He really hated being an instrument of pain for his family. Sal and Diane cried over leaving Jacob and the house. In the end, the joint custody worked fairly well, although Sal never forgave her parents for separating her from her brother during the school year.

As for Katherine, her soon to be ex-husband phoned Diane to claim that he'd had trouble with Katherine before, that she'd been seeking a younger, more virile man for some time. "Well, it appears she found him," Diane reflected.

Diane hoped she could find somebody in the future who was like Laverne, but younger. Laverne had been everything Steve was not, business oriented, yet loving music and the arts. Tough, yet living every moment thinking of Diane, tender when it mattered. Rather than pointing out her faults, he genuinely thought well of Diane, and it was a welcome shock to her system. He had seen life at its worst. Diane knew that made a difference, a keen difference that was important. Laverne loved acutely. Diane did not realize how difficult it would be to find a younger version of Laverne.

Section Three: Snippets 49-71
Chicago and Afar (1982-2003)

49. At Marshall Field's
Chicago, 1982
James and Diane

James, a rising young executive, made his first trip to America in time to watch Macy's Thanksgiving Day Parade in New York, realizing only then why it had been so difficult to book appointments that week. Soon afterward, he visited the fantastic city of Chicago. The skyscrapers amazed him. On a brisk Saturday, with the day to himself, he chose to wander downtown to the iconic Marshall Field's department store on State Street. Christmas decorations were up inside and outside in the windows, a truly amazing experience that left James feeling as if he'd been transported to heaven's gate. In the cosmetics and fragrance section, he chuckled to himself. If only he had a wife who would appreciate him bringing something back to her. He did not. He had a drunk for a wife, and a newborn baby girl at home in England.

James noticed a tall blonde woman about his age experimenting with make-up at the glass display counter. It fascinated him.

"She really doesn't need any make-up," he thought. He could not resist. He was an engaging man and a jokester. He sidled up next to the woman and asked, "What shade do I need?" The woman laughed and said, "Ooohhh, I love that English accent." He got that reaction often. "Well, good day," he said, and went on his way. He thought to talk to her longer would be odd. Besides, he would only be in America for a short time before returning to England to deal with a bad marriage, two little kids of his own, and three stepchildren.

Diane wished the Englishman had stayed and talked longer. Newly single, nobody she dated had yet ignited in her the passion Laverne had. She wondered if she would ever find Laverne's younger version.

Back from a visit to the River, as she called her mother's cottage on Davenport's east side, she just missed seeing Fred and Willetta,

Willie, as Ione's dear friend was affectionately referred to. The women had been close since the Forties, and while Diane was there, Ione projected concern for her old friend without ceasing.

Diane could always tell when her mother was truly upset and asked her what was wrong. Ione explained she'd gone upstairs and found Willie lying so still she thought Willie was unconscious. She put her ear to Willie's mouth to make sure her friend was breathing.

At the end of the visit, when Fred pulled away from the curb outside Ione's house, Ione wondered if she would ever see Willie again.

She would not.

In the Forties, Ione and Willie were the same age as Diane was right after the divorce. Diane mused that she had plenty of life left to live. Perhaps there would yet be time to find the right person for her.

50. The Accident
South Chicago, January 1983
Richard and Mary, Joseph and Lillian

Richard was tired after working all night to fix a college computer system out in Indiana. At this point, his overtime really bordering illegal, he needed to make a meeting in Downers Grove, but took the time to divert south on Interstate 394, knowing Mary was at her aunt's house baking. He planned to stop by, say hello and maybe swipe some baked goods before his meeting. Besides, it was sometimes better to see Mary away from their house and the constant hubbub of their kids.

With the final stop light coming up near the end of the expressway, traveling fast, Richard noticed a truck by the side of the road about to pull out.

What? He was so sleepy. Did he imagine it?

Richard slammed into the rear of a stopped State of Illinois truck at full speed. Soon, paramedics arrived on the scene. Word spread quickly that a fire department lieutenant was inside the car. The situation looked hopeless. The car engine smoldered in the front seat. Rescuers used the Jaws of Life to extricate Richard, who was wedged into the top of the car.

A doctor straddled Richard's chest all the way to the nearest hospital. Then Richard was air-lifted to another hospital where a heart team had been assembled. The paramedics told each other there was no way Richard was going to make it. He'd initially been conscious, giving the responders directions how to get him out. But even then, his situation did not look good.

Lillian and Joseph had just retired to their lake house. Joseph drove like a crazy man and made the south side of Chicago in a few hours. They were in shock at the thought of losing their only son, their only child. Mary was there to meet them, and she too was in shock.

Richard, his aorta hanging by a thread, required emergency surgery to replace the damaged artery with a few inches of pig aorta. It would be months before he was really coherent again. In his mind, Richard created an alternate reality and scared his family to death when he began to regain his senses. The expert medical team lacked time to study prior to the emergency surgery. While clamping off arteries to save Richard's life, blood supply to the spine was destroyed as a consequence. He awoke a paraplegic.

He was angry that he had no say in the decision to choose paralysis over death. He would rather be dead, which destroyed Joseph. There was no consoling Richard. Lillian was strong, but the outcome of the terrible accident took her breath away.

Mary simply didn't know what to do. Richard had taken care of everything. Their marriage would not survive this. When Richard finally did come home, he was like a visitor-patient in the living room. His wife climbed the stairs alone to their bedroom, a room he would not see for years to come. He was intensely angry that so many decisions were made without his input.

Many years later, one of Richard's coworkers wrote a letter to Richard's second wife, a woman he married after being confined to a wheelchair.

Hello Diane,

We met on one or more occasions but I don't think you would remember me. Richard and I worked together as District Specialists. I remember when we were at Hitachi Data Systems (then NAS) and I first learned of his accident. I felt guilty for a long time for my first reaction: a surge of relief that it wasn't me. We shared the account in South Bend for problems at Reliance Electric and Purdue and I remember many nights when I fought to stay awake on the trip down and back. I once worked forty hours straight in South Bend and picked up a hitchhiker on the expressway ramp, told him to get in the driver's side and wake me at O'Hare. Richard's fate could very well have been mine. That aside, Richard was a constant inspiration to all of us with his determination to live his life as he saw fit and not give in to limitations that would have humbled lesser people. Seeing Richard carrying on kind of put our problems into perspective.

I was touched that you shared so many aspects of your life so articulately with us. I hope that you find comfort in those things that comfort us in these times and let your grief surface and pass as grief will. We all have gained who knew Richard and we all have lost something we cannot replace with his passing. Richard represented what we all would like to be if our circumstances required it. His life was a monument to the strength and capacity of the human will. Thank you for sharing your personal insights and feelings. I wish you well and want you to know that many of us share your loss.
Warren M.

Richard lived in a wheelchair for more than twenty years. He passed away in the fall of 2003, his fifty-eighth year. The death certificate listed cause of death as "automobile accident".

51. The Esplanade
New Orleans, 1984
Diane

Diane was enamored with the Crescent City, New Orleans, a soul-center for her. She bought a time-share condo at the eastern edge of the French Quarter near Esplanade and Royal, the old, wealthy Creole section. Esplanade Ridge was actually high ground, so to speak, in New Orleans, most of which sits below sea-level. Her unit, a second floor balcony, featured resplendent, romantic Spanish wrought iron.

She imagined herself here with Laverne and knew it would not be. He had his duties and she was supposed to be finding his younger version. Soon, New Orleans became her escape from Chicago. She hated the cold weather, but Ione needed her up north and now Diane had established a following as a kitchen designer in Chicago's western suburbs. The schools were great for her daughter Sal. And Jacob loved playing little league baseball in Chicago in the summer. Her television buzzed with Cubs games as her son soaked in the Chicago baseball scene.

Ione had been out in Iowa for almost twenty-five years. Her second husband had Alzheimer's disease. Things were pretty challenging on that side of life, but Iowa was only a short drive.

In Chicago, Diane dated a Tom Selleck look-alike. *Tom* wanted children, but Diane was done with that. *Tom* had to leave Diane's place in the middle of the night because Steve called to announce that Katherine had left him. She would lose custody of her kids, of course. There were problems. Steve was a mess on the phone. After *Tom* left, Diane was tempted to throw Sal in the car and just go home and fight for her old life. She missed her home.

Diane had then wondered what her old life really was. If she went back, she would have to deal with Laverne again as well. She stayed up the rest of the night, walking back and forth to Sal's room, staring at the young girl sleeping. The adjustment and hardship had been so difficult for this brave child. But in the end, Diane could not do it. She could not settle.

A few days after the late night call, Katherine returned to Steve and they moved forward together. Time had stepped along. And Diane was dating other men.

Diane's old high school friend, Sue, had helped her with her relocation efforts. Through Sue, Diane met another woman named Christine. Because Sue was so busy with her recent engagement, Diane spent much time with Christine. Both women were no nonsense types. Petite, attractive, Christine escaped being a mafia wife by a thread. Like Diane, she preferred the company of men and never lacked for male attention. Diane did not like many women, but Christine was different. She did not have a husband or children, so she did not spend time complaining about such! Diane found a kindred spirit in Christine and enjoyed spending time with her.

Diane continually attracted younger men who wanted what Diane called, "the original set-up", that is, their first marriage and children. It just didn't work. None of them had Laverne's savvy or swagger. No passion ignited to speak of. She had underestimated her love for Laverne, and she could not replace it. Whenever she drove to Wisconsin for her daughter to spend time with her Dad and brother, Diane would see Laverne again. But it wasn't quite the same. They both knew there was no happy ending on the path they had chosen. Laverne wanted

23. Diane in 1984, still in love with Laverne.

marriage, but Diane could not imagine him raising young children, and she feared that Laverne's daughter Janet would not support the marriage. In that case, Laverne would have lost contact with his grandchildren. In the end, Diane could not be the instrument of destruction. She could not be like Katherine. Diane viewed Katherine as a selfish woman concerned only with her own happiness over that of many other people. She and Diane were just not cut from the same cloth at all. There were times, though, when Diane wondered if Steve and Katherine had been right – get what you want, don't settle – at all cost.

Diane thought of all these things as she leaned over the balcony, soaking in the smell of flowers and the unique spice of the Crescent City. This was like home to her. Sal would learn to love it as well over the years to come. She wondered if Sue and Christine would enjoy New Orleans. Musing, Diane could picture Christine getting lost in the artistry of the Quarter. Diane had changed since she knew Christine; she was worldlier. Things were very different now than when she lived in Wisconsin, had coffee with her friend Lea, and dealt with children all day.

52. Moving on

England, 1985

James, Patricia, Joanne and Alfred

James finally left his wife the drunken day that was one day too many. He eventually had every other weekend with the kids; a custody battle ensued that would endure over a decade. The authorities, disgustingly, were afraid of what the mother would do if the kids were taken from her. He dated. He was attracted to a woman named Patricia, but early on she expressed her desire for a baby. He'd had a vasectomy, which stood in the way, and he ended the relationship. Two weeks later, Patricia was on his doorstep, apparently choosing him over a baby. He didn't bother divorcing his wife; there were constant family issues. He and Patricia simply chose to be together. He started his own business, with which she assisted. Money rolled in. They bought a house and expanded it. The children loved the home. The couple would pick up the kids, who were always dirty. He and Patricia would let them run in the backyard and get dirtier, then they would ritualistically make them squeaky clean.

James' mother, Joanne, simply did not get along with Patricia, and James could not make it better. Joanne saw something that James could not, Patricia's tendency to be possessive.

Joanne was fairly serene now. The children's teenage years had been difficult for Joanne, and the children, grown-up, were all out of the house. She and Alfred had never settled when they found each other; now they had time for themselves and to enjoy grandchildren coming along. Their only concern was James, for he had married the vilest of women and had finally left, but he still had to deal with her. Even though he had started a life with another woman, the battle over the kids continued.

53. Frog Kissing, not Letting Go of the Prince
Chicago, 1988
Diane, Ione, Sal

Diane was fed-up with kissing frogs. She had a bout with early cervical cancer, lived with a man who turned out to be an alcoholic, and spent way too much time with a young widower still in mourning for his wife, who also seemed to drink too much. The experience with an alcoholic was an eye-opener. She got some counseling and joined a support group. Finally, Diane did the work really needed back in 1982. She dealt with her feelings about her divorce and the destruction of their beautiful family home. It was important. Diane needed coping skills. She had Ione, her mother, widowed again, living in the same house for three years. Diane had helped her close out the house in Iowa, settle-up with her stepdaughters, and move her personal belongings to Diane's new home. They purchased furniture together, one of the few times she and her mother had been able to agree. Ione, incapable of seeing two sides to anything, became visibly upset if Diane disagreed with her. Ione was happy to be back in Illinois, especially near Chicago. Diane took her to see 1348 Argyle Street in the city, which made Ione's eyes fill with tears.

Ione had been a Godsend, on one hand. Diane's hours were demanding – how nice it was to have Ione cook and be there for Sal when she came in. Sal worked hard and Diane had given her also the little bit of child support that joint custody had afforded to them until she was eighteen. Sal managed her own budget, as well as school and her causes. With Sal, there were always causes. When Sal believed in something, she really believed. Like her grandmother, she had a tough time seeing two sides to anything. Diane was always in the middle with her shades of gray thinking. Diane was like Harry. Harry was known for answering the phone with catch phrases like, "Duffy's Tap." Diane had an answering machine that asked, "Who do you want, the brunette, the blonde or the red head?"

On the other hand, Ione was her usual intrusive self. Diane was thirty-eight years old, but Ione still suffocated her. They kept Sal at home for the first year of college. She did exceedingly well at the local college, but she planned to attend school in Wisconsin so she could spend time with her father and her brother. Because Steve lived in Wisconsin, Sal had the right to in-state tuition.

Diane decided to take the bull by the horns, as Harry liked to say. Both her girlfriends had moved away, which saddened Diane. Sue and her husband had a small child now. He was promoted and they moved to California. Christine married one of the air traffic controllers laid off by President Reagan. He was in the world of insurance now and bound for Connecticut. With Sal almost out the door, Diane joined an interchurch dating service she learned about through the support group. The only profile she cared for (an ex-Purdue linebacker who liked flowers, dolls, and music) turned out to belong to a man named Richard, who on the second phone call told her about his circumstances. He was in a wheelchair. Diane expected this man had been turned down a lot. She really liked him on the phone and decided there was nothing wrong with being friends. He was an only child also. That alone was worth talking about!

***

It was chilly as Diane drove Sal to Wisconsin to start school. Once there, she saw Laverne again. They were not capable of letting go of each other, it seemed. Yet, he was older, a bit tired-looking. He had started his own business with another old cohort, Bob. Janet was working for him. True to his word, he had no other woman with him in the business. He had said he could not tolerate any other woman, besides his own daughter, working there.

When he heard about her treatment at the hands of the alcoholic, Laverne's face went ashen.

"Diane, I wanted to marry you. None of this would have happened. You did not need to do any of this," Laverne said, almost wearily.

Maybe he had been right, Diane thought, and she wrong. At any rate, it was too late now for him to start over. He was nearing retirement age. "Laverne," she stated simply, "I just would not do that to you at that point, or at this point. Why turn your life upside-down at this age?"

He knew she was right. When he was young, he thought he would set the world on fire. That had not happened. It had been a slow burn in the end. He would continue to do his duty to his family. Laverne lived for Janet's kids. They meant everything to him. He loved being a Grandpa. If he could just do that and go to the Indy 500 every year, he would be happy. He was not a world traveler, and he did not want to travel anywhere with Barbara. He had seen enough of Europe. He would settle for what he had, but in his mind, he had it all with Diane.

"Come on," he said. "Hold your warm and tender body next to mine one more time." Diane, approaching forty, wondered where it had all gone wrong, but Laverne was only in the moment. He had loved her for ten years, and just her touch made him ready for sex, even though he was sixty-four years old.

She lay in his arms again, eyes closed again. Laverne stared at her face for a while, then his mind wandered back to Germany, to Erika. He had only known true passion these two times in his life, but perhaps it was twice more than some ever get. He was a lucky man, really. It hurt him to know that Diane had been with men who were not good enough for her; hell, it hurt that she was with anybody. He had stopped with women; nothing could ever compare for him and he was too old to think about it anymore. Damn this age difference. He couldn't expect her to do anything other than what she was doing.

Diane returned to Chicago where she and Ione busied themselves cleaning out the house a bit. They piled items on the curbside for pick-up. Oddly, Diane noticed the photo of Grandpa Frank Craig on top of the pile, in the glossy oval convex glass framed with ribbons of walnut. When she queried Ione about it, Ione simply replied, "It's time for that awful thing to go." Diane felt a chill, but did not question Ione.

54. Marriage. Settling?
Chicago Heights, 1990
Richard and Diane; their guests

There was something always childlike and innocent about Richard. Diane thought him to be the most honest person she had ever known. He had told her about swiping pies from his Nana Volcker; she thought that was probably the extent of any crime spree by Richard. He played by the rules. His divorce had been hard on him, but he felt that Mary never really let him back in. She left him on a bed in the living room and climbed the stairs to their old bedroom; he had been a patient, not a husband. Looking back later, Richard would say he was so unhappy with his circumstances that he was very difficult to be around. By the time Diane knew him, he had made his adjustments. He didn't show others that the wheelchair was a problem.

Diane and Richard were drawn together by similarities - both being an only child, for starters. "It takes one to understand one," Richard had said. Their fathers both served food to the public, and their mothers worked in a more technical environment (except for Ione's foray into fashion). Still, Ione later returned to the government, working on one of the new computer systems at the Rock Island Arsenal. She felt like she was going to Illinois every day as she ventured out into the middle of the Mississippi River to work. She had trained well and was meticulous, obsessive, in the accuracy of her work.

Yet, the family system of this purely German family was a jolt to Diane. They were loud and very firm in their opinions, unyielding really. There were times Diane felt like she did with Steve's family, a misfit, and too liberal in her thinking. Diane thought in shades of gray. She liked to look at everything from many sides, considering. Richard said she never did get to a black or white moment!

Nevertheless, Richard asked Diane to marry him. He had been in the wheelchair for six years at the time, and he carefully explained all the realities to her. Diane would have to think. A few days later,

Diane was driving along near her own home when the road was blocked and she had to turn around. Upon turning, she saw and felt drawn to a small book store. As if she were being controlled by a heavenly remote device, she parked and went into the store. Again she felt drawn and wound up in the family section. Her eyes fell on a book with a lovely couple on the front. She picked it up and looked at the cover. Opening, she read the preface … a love story. Diane turned the page and saw the full photo of the couple. The man sat in a wheelchair, the woman sat on his lap, grinning. Diane felt nervous inside, strange. She made her way to the front and paid for the book. The *Tom and Ginny* book [6] became legendary in her marriage to Richard. It sat on a shelf as a reminder of the amazing blocked road and book that helped Diane overcome her fears of marrying Richard. Still, she would three times save his life in the future, rushing him to the hospital with bad life-threatening infections. He would sometimes show Diane how much he hated his circumstances, but he never showed his fear.

They wed on the back deck of Richard's Victorian home, with Richard Jr. standing up for his father. Diane's friend Ann was matron of honor. Both Ione and Ione's best friends, Ardis and Roy Wilson, were there that day. Jacob gave his mother away the day after he turned eighteen. Sal flew in from New York, where she was doing an internship. But the happiest man there that day had to be Joseph. He was so very excited for his son and celebrated heartily. The old man had done more than anybody else to help them get ready for the wedding. He brought Lillian from the lake; they did not want to miss a moment. Everything was geared to Richard's comfort. They had a party that spread out from the deck to the dining room. Ione had her own apartment now near where Diane's house had been, but there was also a room for her at Richard's home if needed. Richard bought a special bride doll because it reminded him of Diane, honey-colored hair and all.

Diane had called Laverne when she and Richard were engaged. The conversation was short and Laverne wished her well. Diane shook as she put the phone down. She had not been able to find the younger version of Laverne, but she was happy.

---

[6] *Waiting Hearts*, by Tom and Ginny Carr, 1989, Harold Shaw Publishers.

55. Royal Albert Hall
London, England, 1990
James Hughes

James Hughes prepared to take the stage at Royal Albert Hall for the last time. As a classical harmonica virtuoso, he had amazed crowds for many years. But he was at retirement age now and the trips into London were wearing. His mind wandered back to Ernst, the German who had given him his first harmonica. He smiled that the simple act had changed his life so much. It had been a big sacrifice, certainly, for Ernst, who must have seen something in Jimmy. Jimmy's mind wandered to his sister Joanne and his namesake, James. He loved his family and would dedicate this last performance to all of them, most certainly to his wife.[7]

---

[7] James' protégé, Philip Achille, played for the Andrew Lloyd Webber birthday celebration at Hyde Park, London, in 2008 and played with Lionel Ritchie in 2012.

56. Christmas
On the Road, 1990
Diane, Jacob, Sal

Diane planned a marathon trip to New York just before Christmas. Sal finished her internship but decided not to stay for the next semester. She wanted to get back to Wisconsin. Matthew, Sal's brilliant boyfriend, would join her in Chicago for Christmas.

Diane just knew she had to get all Sal's stuff in her car and get home for Christmas. Diane still worked for the kitchen firm in the west suburbs. She had to take significant time off to run out to New York and back, but it was the slow time of year for kitchen sales.

Diane was one for planning elaborate logistics. In college, Sal had devised a stand-up comedy act all about it, which was hilarious. Diane realized there was not enough time for this trip and that the car would have to go straight through to New Jersey. Richard did not want Diane driving through the night alone, but it was impossible for him to make such a trip. Jacob rode along instead.

The scheduled meet-up was at the home of Sal's ex-boyfriend, Jonathan, in New Jersey. He lived with his family and attended Rutgers. This saved Diane and Jacob from driving into the city. Sal had attended Hunter College on a political science internship. She had worked at the U.N. and briefly spoke on the phone to Mikhail Gorbachev when he was President of the Soviet Union. While Sal worked there, Ardis and Roy Wilson, who had gone to New York for the theater, took Sal to dinner.

Diane's plan included flying Jacob from Minneapolis to Cleveland to help with the driving through the night. Then he too could spend Christmas in Chicago. Diane was at the Cleveland airport only to discover snow in Minneapolis delayed Jacob's flight. Diane hated having family fly in snow. It really made her nervous. Jacob was still her baby boy to her, even if he was eighteen. Jacob stood 6'4" and was as handsome as could be with those brilliant *Ione* eyes.

Some of Ione's characteristics had finally shown up in Jacob, at least her coloring. The war was on in Iraq. A group of soldiers, Vietnam vets included, were on Jacob's plane. They were coming home for Christmas, then leaving for Iraq. Diane talked to a woman in dire straits with her husband deployed. Diane gave her $50 and asked her to go out to dinner with her husband. The television station was there to greet these men.

When Jacob finally arrived, after a couple of hours' delay, he blinked at the flashing lights of the media as he left the jet-way. Diane threw him in the car and they were off. The plan was for Jacob to drive through the night, which meant traversing the wide state of Pennsylvania. Diane awoke to Jacob exclaiming something. He had just noticed the gas was almost gone. They took the next exit; all was closed. The following exit was circuitous, but they finally wound up at a gas station that looked open; bundled men were actually on rockers on the front porch. They informed Diane that they were diesel only. Diane had never heard of a diesel-only gas station! There were no other stations, so back onto the turnpike they went. Another car had tailed them into the gas station. It was a group of Middle Eastern students with the same problem. They continued following Diane and Jacob.

"This is just great," stated Jacob. "It's the middle of the night, no gas. Those gas station guys looked like they were out of the movie *Deliverance* and I have the Iraqis on my tail."

Diane thought she would keel over laughing. Jacob had Steve's sardonic sense of humor. At least they were on the highway. If they ran out of gas, maybe the highway patrol would get them before they died at the hands of the students!

Jacob took the next exit. They were out of options. It was almost time for the normal looking gas station to open for the day. Neither of them were even clear as to why Sal wanted to exit the program and not complete the second semester in New York- but they were on the way to rescue her. In reality, Sal had her first affair with a woman, but of course, her family did not know this, certainly not her boyfriend Matthew. She had been fascinated for some time. The fascination eventually crossed the line, and it did not end well. Sal just wanted to get back to people she knew. She needed to see Matthew and figure everything out.

57. Victorian House and the Lake House
Chicago Heights, 1992
Richard, Diane, Ione, Sal and Jacob

Richard and Diane had remodeled the old Victorian home south of Chicago. Outfitted with ramps and lifts for Richard, post-accident, it was obvious they needed to live there after all that had been done to the house. Diane designed a kitchen to make Richard's life easier, and to express her design tastes. It was a bit exhausting, as Diane continued to drive back and forth to the west suburbs to her job, which was a three hour round trip daily. Richard drove the Tri-State expressway daily as well. He was an expert with hand controls. Finally, Richard had suggested she just start her own independent business out of the house. It made sense.

The couple looked forward to coming home to their Golden Retriever, the dog Richard had adopted right before he met Diane. The dog's name was Jedi, and he was devoted to the big man in the wheelchair. Two cats were also in residence, Midi, a coal black cat, and Blu, a Russian Blue. The cats would never live elsewhere. They ended their days in the Victorian house.

Diane and Richard sometimes fought. Diane had lost trust in men, and she projected some of that distrust onto Richard. Of course, Richard had that temper to deal with, which was even more hair-trigger after being confined to a wheelchair.

Often, they would travel to a lake district several hours away where Lillian and Joseph were retired. As a wedding present, Lillian and Joseph gave them the lot next door to their house. Diane had drawn plans, and Richard was starting to execute them with local tradesmen. Diane and Richard viewed the house as their eventual retirement home. Diane had designed it while touring Sonoma during one of Richard's business trips. She made Richard stop by the side of the road while she sketched a house high on a hill. She also sketched many of the wineries. By the end of the day, Diane took over driving. Richard was a bit tipsy, unusual for him. Medically, drinking was unadvisable.

Their lake house would have a deck all around for Richard to enter the house on any side he wished. The house wasn't ready yet when Ione's eightieth birthday rolled around. All she wanted, she said, was to go to the Andy Williams Theater in Branson, Missouri. Friends and family organized the party in the summer before Ione's November birthday. Jokes abounded about her then actually living to see eighty. Diane organized an elaborate party. Ardis and Roy Wilson came down from Iowa, and of course, Lillian and Joseph, Richard's parents, came along. Sal and Jacob were not thrilled about making the trip, but they didn't have a choice, it was Grandma Ione's eightieth birthday party. Diane drove through Illinois, picking up her Aunt Magna and Aunt Mary, Hope's grandmother, along the way. Aunt Magna, now a widow, sat beside Reverend Bernard's bed every day until he died.

Not long after the party, Diane traveled out east to give a talk for a seminar. She prepared diligently and was rehearsing in her hotel room when a knock came at the door and she was greeted with a dozen yellow roses. They had been sent by a girlfriend to wish her luck. She immediately called her friend, who laughed and asked, "Are they pretty red and white carnations like I ordered?"

"No," said Diane slowly, staring at the roses. "They are yellow roses."

"That's odd," said her friend Ann. "I definitely ordered carnations." Tears rolled down Diane's face. She excused herself to repair makeup prior to her talk. The yellow roses meant that Harry had made his presence known.

Things were rolling along; Sal was finishing up college and had been elected President of the student body. She was engaged to the newspaper editor, Matthew. Suddenly, at least from Diane's viewpoint, Sal announced she was gay. Diane was furious that she would do this to Matthew. After all, Diane had envisioned white picket fences and grandchildren. She drove to Wisconsin to see Sal. Surely she must be wrong. Surely she was going to marry Matthew.

Things did not go well. Sal was as down your throat as her father always was, and Diane was so mad about Matthew. Of course, the reality was that this was not sudden, but borne out of hours and hours of soul searching and world experience for Sal. Breaking Matthew's heart was the worst experience of her young life.

Still upset, Diane drove back Chicago. In the car, she started thinking about Ione and how she never really appreciated men. Ione once described her relationship with Harry as, "we both had a low sex drive." Diane was always surprised she even made it into the world. In a flash, she realized that Ione was probably, had it been at all popular or acceptable in her day, tending towards lesbianism. She had always made Diane feel unacceptable for having a healthy interest in men.

"My God," Diane thought to herself, "that's what I have done to Sal!"

Diane felt a wave of acceptance wash over her, not only for Sal, but for poor Ione, who probably had no clue. It was a spiritual wash of love. In weeks to come, Ione would be hospitalized and sedated. Under the influence of drugs, she would go on and on about the pretty nurses, and Sal would just look at Diane with raised eyebrows.

Sal went off to New Orleans to start over, without Matthew and far away from family. Matthew was heartbroken. After his year at Northwestern to obtain his master's degree, he left for Hong Kong.

58. Ellie!
England, 1994
James, Patricia, Ellie

James reflected. Things had been good for many years now; life had a pattern, even if he had never won custody of his two kids. The authorities were afraid of what Catrine would do if she lost the kids. He had put an addition on his house to bring the office in and Patricia helped him run the public relations company; they had many large accounts with home builders. Just when he thought all was well, Patricia became unhappy because she had never had that baby of her own. She was despondent over it and James agreed to attempt a vasectomy reversal. He remained very concerned, however, about any change in family dynamics.

Patricia became pregnant. Elinor, "Ellie", was born. At first, there had been slaps on the back all around regarding this success. But in time, long after he already loved Ellie, James contemplated his doctor's questions about whether he had even fathered the child. The doctor just didn't think it possible.

As if the doubts were not bad enough, Patricia had changed dramatically after Ellie's birth. James had finally divorced Catrine and married Patricia prior to Ellie's birth. He wanted Patricia to feel secure as a mother. But everything went upside-down. Patricia paid no attention to the other children, nor to James. She focused completely on Ellie as if she were a new possession. She swaddled Ellie in an unusual manner because of a skin rash and could not, would not, achieve any sort of balance. She no longer helped James with the business, despite ongoing promises, and he was stressed both personally and professionally.

59. Starting New Things
New Orleans and South of Chicago, 1994
Diane, Sal

Diane visited Sal in New Orleans. But she was on tenterhooks. If she could secure an SBA loan from a Chicago bank, she would be able to open her showroom in the Chicago Merchandise Mart after being approached by a major player in the kitchen industry.

Hanging out with Sal in Sal's single shotgun in Uptown, New Orleans, was Diane's way of waiting for news about her loan application. Sal was exploring her new gay life in the Crescent City, working at a doll shop in Jackson Square during the day and bartending at the women's bar some nights and weekends. Sal had always been good at saving and managing money.

Diane was on board with Sal's sexual orientation. She even went to a meeting of the *Lesbian Avengers* and made business suggestions. That same night, Sal tended bar. Diane was a lightweight when it came to drinking. After just one of Sal's special Bloody Marys, she was a bit tipsy. Not thinking about where she was, Diane danced a bit to a tune she liked, just tripping along by herself. She was Harry and Ione's daughter, after all. Well, there was a woman, a scary-looking woman, who took a shine to Diane. Sal came across the bar and let the woman know a thing or two, saying, "That's my mother, leave her alone!"

Often people were incredulous that Diane could be Sal's mother. Her youthful skin was a blessing passed on from Ione, smooth, not a wrinkle to be found. Of course, Diane and Sal were only nineteen years apart in age.

When Sal and Diane returned to the shotgun, there was a message from Chicago. Two banks were interested. Diane had her money. It was time to celebrate. Diane invited Sal to come back to Chicago and work in the Chicago Merchandise Mart. Sal said she would think about it. It was always difficult for either of them to leave New Orleans. Of course, Ione was now past eighty years old and needed both of them, which contributed to Sal's eventual decision to move back north.

Not long after returning to their Victorian home way south of Chicago, Diane realized Richard was not doing well. A new infection raged inside of him. He had an open sore, and Diane could see it turning color. They fought into the middle of the night when Richard refused to go to the hospital. Diane finally cried and cried so he relented. Once there, the doctors wondered if he would live to see the next day.

Plans were well under way for the showroom. Corporate executive officers were due to arrive in Chicago. Kindly, considering Richard's condition, they arranged to drive south to meet Diane. She raced to meet them at a nice restaurant near the hospital. Diane managed to pull herself together to get through the meeting. She could tell the Vice President of Sales and Marketing was relieved to see she could do this while Richard was so ill. Richard's recovery was up and down. Diane had to make trips into the Chicago Merchandise Mart and then quickly drive back south. She would drive the Dan Ryan Expressway wondering what she would find once at the hospital. Diane raced in the door as fast as her high heels would take her. She found Richard feverish and also quite upset. What was wrong?

"Diane," he said, "Mary was here today. My fever started raging and I just let her talk." Richard always worried about upsetting his ex-wife. Mary's sister committed suicide after her own divorce and Richard feared Mary might follow suit. "She had a whole theory about why we got divorced. I was so sick, I did not know what to say, so I just let her talk," Richard continued. "Diane, I am so upset. I think she left here thinking we are still in love. Of course, she was upset seeing me like this. You know I love you, right Diane?"

"Of course I do, Richard," Diane responded. Privately she wanted to strangle the woman. How dare she upset Richard like this when he was so ill?

Soon, Richard Jr. and his wife, Polly, called to figure out what was going on. They were under the impression that Richard and Mary were getting back together.

"No," Diane carefully explained. "Richard was in a fog of fever and he just let her talk. He was quite upset about the whole thing when I got there."

"Yeah, we figured it was something like that," Richard Jr. stated. "Mom really convinced herself of the truth of it."

Diane hung up, shaking her head. Diane brought Richard home, after fighting with him to save his life. The antibiotics worked that time.

60. The Showroom
Chicago Merchandise Mart, 1995-96
Diane and Richard, Sal

Diane and Sal opened the showroom after a frantic build-out. They had a few design-types to help them out. Sal would learn to price kitchens and start from the bottom. She had a knack for showing people plan cost options; the clients liked it. This information gave them control over their finances and decisions. In addition, her natural artistic talent allowed her to package beautiful finishes with the appropriate granites and tiles. It would not be long until Sal would move into sales and saved enough money from commissions to buy her first home on the expanding north side of Chicago.

Sal was excited. It was a *three-flat*. She could rent out the upper and lower levels and live in the middle. The house was scheduled to appreciate fast due to its neighborhood north of Wrigley Field. Sal closed on the house on a Chicago December day, and the family went over to see her open the door, Ione included. A single yellow rose was in full bloom at the bottom of the steps. Sal was the one person who understood the yellow rose and made comment about Harry being present.

Richard continued to work in the computer industry and, as was his usual conservative way, he felt he should keep working there while the showroom went through start-up. He was so happy at the grand opening. He wore the suit he had worn at his wedding; he wanted Diane to wear her dress, but it was white and inappropriate according to Diane. Ione, eighty-two years old, attended the grand opening and loved every minute of it. Richard Jr. was there with his family. Only Jacob could not make it down from school.

Expensive tile and granite adorned the high-styled cabinetry. Lighting sparkled on it all. The Vice President of the factory had been on a stepladder the day before painting a hood. So many people contributed.

In reality, Jacob was in the middle of something. He had earlier broken up with the only girl he ever talked to his mother about, Kallista Waters. It was his own fault. He had been immature, drinking, partying. Jacob was not quite what she was looking for in a man, so Kallista broke it off and began seeing an older man. In fact, Jacob couldn't get over her. When he heard she was pregnant, he called his mother and counted months. Clearly, the baby was not his. He was angry.

But the months ticked away, and Kallista did some real soul-searching. She decided she could not marry the baby's father. They were all wrong for each other. But she wanted the baby. She wrote to Jacob and told him she felt they made a mistake breaking up, that they had something special. She was rewarded for her honesty. Jacob essentially became baby Aaron's father. He and Kallista moved in together and planned their future.

Jacob didn't know how to tell his parents about all this. What would they think? When he called Diane, she listened intently. Indeed, Kallista was the only girl he had ever mentioned to his mother. The tall handsome man had certainly known other girls, but Diane didn't know the details, of course. Jacob had many of Harry's characteristics, a real bent when it came to business. Diane felt he was young but stable emotionally.

"Jacob," she said, "it is not an ideal circumstance, but you might as well know now that very few things in life are ideal." Diane's thoughts flashed to Laverne. Indeed, very few things.

61. Fall Wedding

Wisconsin 1996

Jacob and Kallista, Aaron, Diane and Richard, Sal and Ione

The whole family came together in Wisconsin to see Jacob and Kallista married. Sal was an uncomfortable bridesmaid. It was too *foo-foo* for her. She did not look forward to seeing Steve's mother, who disapproved of Sal. Ione looked forward to the event and traveled with Diane and Richard or in Sal's car, which suited her.

Kallista was gorgeous; Jacob looked so happy. He, like Harry, the grandfather he never knew, was a stable family-type man. Diane knew he would do well. He was conquering his studies and would soon enter the world of software. His major was a combination of business and computer technology. Aaron wore a little tuxedo and was absolutely precious. Not yet two, he handled the ring bearer's job. The following year, the couple would welcome Alexandra into the world. Diane became a grandmother, Ione a great-grandmother.

Diane traveled to be there for Alexandra's birth. She and Kallista tried a few tricks to get the baby into the world and made one trip to the hospital together. Diane delayed a necessary business trip one day, but finally had to leave. Three hours down the road to Chicago, Jacob called to tell her Alexandra had arrived. It would be two weeks before Diane could get back to see her. She was perfect and looked quite a bit like Kallista.

Diane broke away to visit her dear friend, Lea, before heading back to Chicago. The Merchandise Mart showroom was demanding eighty and ninety-hour work weeks from Diane, which would not be sustainable. She missed the days with Lea. They represented a simpler time and place.

62. The Jewelry Box

Hinckley, the Midlands, England, 1997
James, Patricia, Joanne, Ellie

James found a love letter in Patricia's jewelry box. Old or new, he wondered? His doubts increased. She, too, had her doubts. Patricia constantly accused him of having affairs. He just wasn't the type to do that. He really loved being a family man. The ball of yarn of their life just kept unwinding. Things went from bad to worse.

He floundered. He had always been the passionate one in the beginning. Patricia had not matched his passion, and she knew it. That is why she accused him of affairs. She knew he was more intense and sexual than she ever wanted to be. Finally, James asked for a divorce. His children, now teenagers, felt rejected by Patricia. James was having trouble with his elder daughter, Jessie, a wild teen. He once pulled her out of a dance hall dressed in a little teeny skirt she had smuggled out of the house.

Patricia could not bear the embarrassment or any thought of fault, especially when she would talk to her father. She grouped together with her sisters and immediately ostracized James. They told their parents things about him that were untrue in an effort to support Patricia in getting full custody of Ellie. By the time James asked for a paternity test, things were out of control.

"If you touch one hair on her head, I will bring you up on assault charges," Patricia screamed. "My family and I will raise this child. You can see her supervised for four hours a month. That is what is going to happen when I am through with you."

James' mother, Joanne, had never liked Patricia and felt he was a fool to believe the child was his. She thought he should just wipe out the whole episode. Joanne had seen this coming. She was a wise woman, but perhaps too eager to rid the family of Patricia and her offspring. Patricia had been possessive of James. She just did not like sharing him with his family. Patricia had tolerated James' children; she dare not do otherwise. But now, with her own baby, her true colors had come out; that's what Joanne believed to be true. Her possessive nature was in full force when it came to Ellie. Joanne did not believe the baby was her granddaughter, not one bit.

James sold the house and gave the lion's share of their joint estate to Patricia to raise Ellie. He never found out for sure if Ellie was his daughter, but in his heart and on the birth certificate, she certainly was.

Disillusioned, James' eighteen-year-old son Len went to his mother's home, where the environment was far more liberal, to start his own life. Just a short time earlier there had been a home filled with the hustle and bustle of family life. Now it was all gone. James sat in his car and could not move. He called his sister, June, who had moved back to be near him in England, and she rushed to help him. It was the first panic attack he experienced, but not the last.

James never really recovered from the shock. He could not bear to have an unnatural relationship with Ellie; he did not have the fight in him after his earlier custody fight, which had gone on for more than a decade. He did not want to drag Ellie through anything like that. He knew Patricia and her family would love Ellie and give her every advantage. That was not a worry in the least.

"Well," he said to himself, "it seems I have an opportunity to start over in life. America or Singapore?" He could not live in the same country as Ellie and not see her.

63. Fiftieth Anniversary
Chicago, 1997
Diane, Laverne, Janet

Diane slipped into a depression triggered by overworking, and she had no idea that it happened. Her marriage was strained. Richard did not understand the pressure she was under, but they sought help from a counselor named Stan. Her days at the Chicago Mart were long and grueling as she struggled to make the business become viable in two years. Meeting volume requirements meant hiring people, and Diane really did not like managing people. She found employees to be too high-maintenance. With one or two exceptions, they all needed lessons from Laverne. One dear, darling girl had become like a daughter, however, Rachel. She was brilliant.

An impressive-looking envelope arrived at Diane's office from Wisconsin. It was from Janet, but her last name was different and Diane realized she had remarried. Diane opened the envelope and her heart nearly stopped. Janet never knew about Diane loving her father, of course. She was inviting Diane to her father and Barbara's fiftieth wedding anniversary party in Wisconsin. Diane started shaking, not quite believing the effect this was having on her. The roll-over phone lines were all lit up at the showroom, but Diane ignored them. She tucked the envelope in her purse, only to throw it out later. Janet might think her rude. She did not care.

***

In Wisconsin, Laverne suffered through the anniversary party. He played the part, his usual, talkative self. He asked Barbara to dance, even though he knew she would rather dance with her son. Throughout the day, he thought of both Erika and Diane. What if he had stayed in Germany and made a family there? What if he had convinced Diane to marry him at all costs?

He wasn't happy as things were, but he would continue to make the best of it, just as he had for fifty years.

Two different men, "came out of the woodwork," (one of Harry's phrases again), during Diane's tenure at the Mart. They both professed some level of love for her, and both were married. In truth, they both reminded her some of Laverne. She was sorely tempted to have a full-blown affair with one of them after the temper tantrum when Richard smacked her to the floor. At that point, she thought she had made another terrible mistake and seriously considered getting out of the marriage. But in the end, she knew Richard suffered supreme frustration with the wheelchair. Nobody wanted to hurt Richard, not the two men, and certainly not Diane. Everybody could see what a good man he was, and his circumstance was obvious. Neither of the men really wanted to disturb their own lives, and both men became good friends to Diane.

Occasionally, they exchanged words about another place and time. One of them, the one she pushed away most often, really was a younger version of Laverne. He sported the same business savvy, the same ability to evaluate people and their motivations, the same Type-A personality. But he arrived too late. He could help or hurt her career the most. But she kept him at arm's length. Richard never hurt Diane again. He had been mortified. He did not realize his own strength.

Many old friends, especially women, thought Diane had settled for less than she should have with Richard, but Diane learned more from Richard than anybody else she ever knew, other than Laverne. She may have settled for some anger, restrictions and a dose of fear added to her life, but she learned about loyalty, tenacity, survival skills, and sacrifice. And Richard was one of the handsomest men who ever walked – or rode – on this earth. His unbelievable eyes were a true window to his innocent soul. Richard kept buying dolls, *Snow Village* pieces, and model cars. He said he lost so much to paralysis, collecting was something he could do. Diane watched with amazement as he fastened jewelry onto porcelain dolls with his large hands. The cleaning crew lost their minds cleaning the old Victorian house with all the collections …

Richard was part of a massive layoff by his employer. He decided then to help Diane with the business, a good decision. He did not have to hurry in the morning to get ready. Getting ready was a struggle for a while. He learned firsthand what Diane was up against with the business, and it was what she needed from him. Richard was very good at handling money and watching the back end of the business. Diane felt grateful.

64. Arrival in America
Las Vegas, 1997-98
James and Jillian

James landed in California and made his way to Las Vegas. He loved the desert air. What a change from England. Once in a while, he had a panic attack, like in the airport in New York. But for the most part, he was determined to make his way in America.

James worked as a sales representative. He met young Jillian in one of the stores. He was forty-two. She was twenty-six, sixteen years his junior. He wasn't thinking. He had just seen a pair of blue eyes. Jillian's family was nice and welcoming. Maybe this would work.

James built a small but new home in Las Vegas and settled in with Jillian. Her bills were a mess. He cleared that up. He became interested in voice-acting, and soon he was announcing on public television when they aired British comedy. James was as happy as he could possibly be.

65. Special Birthday
Downtown Chicago, November 18, 1998
Diane, Ione, Jacob

Diane and Richard leased an apartment in downtown Chicago, just outside the Mart. Diane worked so many hours that she sometimes had to crash. They also used it on weekends, calling Jedi a special dog, one who assisted the handicapped, in order to gain access for him.

One evening after closing out at the Mart, Diane arrived after 9 p.m. at the apartment. Quite a bit later, the phone rang. Jacob announced that Kallista was in labor for baby number three. "Mom," he said, "it looks like we are going to make Grandma Ione's birthday with this baby."

Diane could not sleep. Finally, morning came and she decided to shower. "That will bring on the phone call," she thought. Indeed it did. Baby Karlin had arrived on her great-grandmother's birthday. Diane's first call was to Ione at her apartment.

Diane could tell she had probably caused Ione to wake up. "Sorry," she said, "but I thought you would want to know your great-granddaughter has just been born on your birthday." Ione was quite emotional at the news, and Diane thought how she would always be celebrating this birthday through her own lifetime.

A couple of weeks later, the news came of Roy Wilson's death in Iowa. Diane took time off from the frantic Merchandise Mart and drove Ione to Iowa for the funeral. Greg Wilson was a lawyer in Des Moines now. Diane remembered the forlorn boy at Harry's funeral. Now he was a strong man, capable of emotionally supporting his whole family.

After the funeral, Diane drove Ione past 2224 N. Clark Street, their first home in Iowa. Diane remembered the flower bed in front that spelled her name the first spring. Ione was so grateful to be sitting outside the house where they had been a family. The owner of the home opened the front door and stepped out. Diane quickly sprang out of the car and joked that they were not casing the joint.

"We were the first owners of this home," she stated to the woman.

"Is that Ione Williams you have there in the car?"

"Well, yes, it is my mother, Ione!" replied Diane.

"Bring her in the house!"

Ione was in heaven. She sat and talked to the people to whom she had sold the house in 1975. Ione had been in the house fifteen years, followed by their nearly twenty-five years. Visiting the house made quite an impact on both Ione and Diane. They remained quiet in the car as they left. Then Ione began crying.

"I didn't appreciate the years we had there together, Diane." she realized.

As the next year wore on, Ione's health began failing. She had several bouts with congestive heart failure. Prednisone was the treatment. After a couple of episodes, Ione turned into somebody Diane could no longer recognize. Her personality was completely altered. The doctors all shrugged their shoulders and one of them said, "Put her in a home."

Diane took her to the Victorian house and tried to deal with this new person. The usual tense and repressed mother now had loose lips. She told crude jokes; not at all like Ione. It was as if a lifetime of repressions were spilling out. That's how Diane found out about what Frank Craig had done to her when she was young. He had touched her inappropriately when she lay dozing on the sofa.

It had been dark. Had he mistaken her for her mother? Ione never knew, but she had carried this, which had been her private terror, around her entire life. "No wonder we threw out that portrait," Diane murmured to herself. Ione also wanted to discuss what she had done to Diane emotionally when she was a child. But of course, Diane knew Ione was in no condition to discuss anything.

Eventually a nurse at an emergency room figured out that Ione was having a reaction to the prednisone. "Prednisone psychosis," she called it. Doctors altered the medication and Diane had the normal Ione back. But she was failing. She was also going blind with macular degeneration and could no longer drive her car.

"It's time I went into an assisted living care facility," Ione announced. "That's what I want."

Diane helped her to find a nice place with a beautiful atrium and dining room. Attached was a nursing home in case that was needed. Indeed, Ione would float between the two, as she would sometimes require oxygen. Ione often used the world albatross. She never wanted to be an albatross.

Ione turned eighty-seven in the home. Diane drove out to take her to dinner that night. As Diane entered Ione's room, she saw a huge spray of yellow roses. Ione pointed to them and said they were from Magna. Neither women knew what yellow roses meant to Diane, but Diane knew that Harry was calling Ione home to be with him. Years before, Ione had experienced her first heart attack - before she had married John T. Ione saw the flat line on the monitor; she felt she was leaving her body. Then she had seen Harry. Harry told her she would be, "going back". He said she still had, "things to do". And she had. She and John T. hosted warm Christmas times at their house for Diane's children. When John T. was diagnosed with Alzheimer's, Ione was kind to him. She did all she could until he could no longer live in their home. Then she drove her car to the special home and would spring him for lunch. Jacob was the last to say good-bye to John T. at the home, the last of Diane's extended family. That was back in 1985. Now, fourteen years later, Harry apparently thought Ione had completed her tasks. It would not be long.

With both Richard and Diane working in the Mart, they were struggling with a disjointed life that spanned from the old Victorian house to the lake house to the apartment and Ione's facility. Diane asked Richard if he would give up the Victorian house and move to a condo downtown so life would be easier. Diane pointed out the amount of time they were spending on expressways, especially with Ione in a home. Richard put it in her hands. If she could find a first floor condo and the bathrooms could be made to work for him, then he would do it. He hated the bathroom at the apartment.

Chicago's west loop was being rebuilt near the Oprah Winfrey studio. Diane found a condo where they could make a few alterations. They captured a good price for the Victorian house. But the move was the biggest mess of Diane's life. Richard had resided there for more than thirty years. They planned a giant garage sale, which brought Mary around. Mary stood in the street and cried while Diane loaded the van like a mule. Yet Diane did feel sympathy for her.

129

It was all worth it. Richard loved the new condo and life was much easier. Even in the winter, he and Diane could drive from their underground parking to the underground parking at the Mart. Even the grocery store had underground parking! Jedi made many new dog friends. The building was full of newlyweds trying out parenthood by having a dog. Richard hoped they could get to the lake more often now.

No sooner had they settled than a phone call came from Wisconsin, Lea's husband, Sam. He told Diane that Lea had cancer and it had spread to her liver. Diane could not speak. She shook and had to put the phone down, excusing herself from Sam. Eventually she and Lea would have long talks. Lea would beat the cancer down, but it would win in the end. On one trip to Chicago, the two couples went out to eat. Lea was allowed to express her feelings to a very understanding Richard. Diane choked back tears, but Lea looked angelic. She had the purest soul Diane had ever known. Lea thanked them. So many of her friends had not been able to talk to her – indeed considered it a lack of faith to do so.

Diane hugged Lea and thought of all the silly talks they used to have over coffee. Some not so silly.

Diane went home and sat with feet up sipping coffee. She had the pink satin handkerchief box in her lap. Ione had given it to her. Diane removed the entire stack of hankies, studied each one, folded them, and put each back in the box.

66. Hellos and Good Byes
New Orleans, 2000
Diane and Richard, James, Ione, Sal, Magna, Joseph

In February, Diane and Richard went to New Orleans. For years, they had traded their timeshare balcony unit for one near the courtyard pool so that Richard could have access. He had become comfortable enough here to enjoy the city with Diane. The rough sidewalks and streets were sometimes difficult in his wheelchair, but Diane would help him if needed. They made their way. It was such a hassle to put Richard in a taxi, so they walked the French Quarter, even at night. Richard's upper body, Diane thought, would be enough to scare off criminals, even in a wheelchair!

One night, out listening to the blues, on their own of course, Diane and Richard struck up a conversation with men at the next table. Among a group of sales representatives in town for meetings, one, a tall Englishman, was most talkative. Diane loved his accent.

James studied Diane. There was something familiar about her. Then he realized she reminded him of the tall blonde he had seen in Marshall Fields years ago. "What year was that? 1982 … in Chicago, my first trip to the USA."

Diane and wheelchair-bound Richard joined their group for the evening. James asked a lot of questions. He always liked to find out what people did for a living. The couple started talking about their business in the Chicago Merchandise Mart … James' mind wandered … Was she the same blonde woman? What were the odds? At some point, James moved near her and sat down. "You know," he said, "I swear you look like a woman I saw many, many years ago. She was trying on makeup at Marshall Fields in downtown Chicago, and I asked her what shade I should use."

Diane turned to look at him. Indeed, such an episode had happened to her when she was newly single and missing Laverne. "I believe that was me," she said. They laughed heartily and discussed odds. Well, anyway, she was married, James thought. And he was living with young Jillian back in Las Vegas. Their business sounded interesting; he took their business card and promised to stay in touch. Maybe he would visit them at the Merchandise Mart sometime.

Diane handed the Englishman her business card, then she and Richard excused themselves. Richard looked tired. They would be leaving in two days. Ione was on Diane's mind. She was in a nursing home. Back in Chicago, Sal was in charge of the showroom and Grandma. Ione was not doing well, but Aunt Magna continued to be healthy and active. Magna lived at a Methodist retirement home southwest of Chicago.

Ione died on April 10th, shortly after Diane's fiftieth birthday. Diane was alone with her at the end, holding her hand and watching her go. Diane knew instantly that she was gone; there was no doubt. Sal had been at the home often, but not the day Ione passed. The redhead lamented the fact, but Diane said, "I don't think it was for grandchildren to be there at that moment."

Diane arranged an all blue casket and planned a service at Ione's church in the suburbs. Then the body was transported to Iowa, where another funeral transpired for old friends and family in Diane's home church. Diane wrote the eulogy, talking about how Ione's male support people had all faded from her life; how fear often had taken over. It was almost thirty years since they had buried Harry with military honors in the national cemetery on Arsenal Island. As Harry's widow again, following John T.'s death, Ione qualified for burial with Harry. They were finally reunited on the island in the middle of the Mississippi River.[8]

At the church, Jacob and Kallista sat in front with all three children. The youngest little girl, Karlin, was born on Ione's birthday in 1998. Aaron and Alexandra found the back stairs to the balcony and made a grand entrance down the sweeping front stairs by the pulpit during the eulogy. They were too cute for words. Karlin, who had shared one birthday with Ione, was on her mother's lap.

Aunt Magna attended the funeral, although Uncle Barney was already gone to be with Harry. Magna even went to the gravesite and walked about gingerly. Then the pastor's widow led the prayers.

---

[8] First Army commander, Lieutenant General Michael S. Tucker, currently serves at the Rock Island Arsenal. He assumed command there August 2, 2013.

Harry's grave had been opened. Diane was ready with a handful of yellow roses. She sprinkled them on Harry's casket. Then Ione's beautiful blue casket was lowered on top as is typical of national cemeteries. Magna held Diane close and remembered the night they almost lost Diane.

"Well, now Diane has lost both of them," thought Magna.

Diane and Richard returned to their condo in the West Loop. The center garden had turned to a field of yellow flowers while they were gone, Diane noted. It was Easter.

Before summer ended, Diane and Richard would also say good-bye to Joseph at the lake. He had soldiered on, taking care of Lillian, who was handicapped and got around with a walker. He had done the cooking and worked as hard as possible, but the end had come. All the days since the zinging Japanese bullet had been bonus to him.

Richard was an excellent driver using hand controls. He had been on his way to the lake when Joseph died. Lillian called Chicago to tell Diane. Diane called to Richard Jr., and they decided to call Richard on his cell phone, to let him know before arriving at the lake. Diane looked at the clock. Her husband would be an hour away. Diane could picture the long stretch of ribbon road from I-70 south to the lake, hilly yet smooth. Diane told Richard Jr., "It should come from me." She called Richard and had him pull over to the side of the road.

"No, no, no ..." he groaned.

Diane could see his big chest heaving through the phone. She so wished she had gone with him. Thank God for Lillian, though, that her only son was so close and would be with her soon. Diane, Richard Jr. and Polly would be on their way as quickly as possible. Richard was not close to his only daughter, but she would come for her grandmother.

67. Vanished
Chicago Merchandise Mart, January 19, 2001
Richard and Diane, Sal

It was the date of Richard's accident, the anniversary, a Friday, just after lunch. Phone calls started rolling into the Mart showroom. People were hysterical. The factory for all the franchises across the country had vanished into thin air. Their website was gone. Phones went unanswered. The large Pennsylvania manufacturer was AWOL.

In the aftermath of the factory bankruptcies and buyouts, Richard and Diane exercised their right to resign. Richard sat in his wheelchair, racked with sobs, as he watched workers demolish the showroom. Diane stayed away. Sal was stunned. She thought they would always have their showroom. Sal's house had doubled in value over the few years she had been at the Mart. She contemplated selling and going back to New Orleans. Ione did not need her any more, she sadly acknowledged, and it would be years until Diane would be elderly.

68. The Day before 9/11
Fall, 2001
Lillian, Richard, Diane

After the factory sold, Richard and Diane worked another year from home to satisfy customers and deliver product with the new ownership. On top of it, Richard's handicapped mother refused to leave her home at the lake, next door to Diane and Richard's house. Family members, nurses, and neighbors were run ragged trying to manage the situation. Richard himself did not look good.

Finally, matters became worse. Lillian had colon cancer and required surgery. The doctor made no promises. For years, her body had been thin from thyroid difficulties and cancer would weaken her considerably. After the surgery, Richard convinced her to take a medical flight to Chicago so that the family could attend to her. Richard Jr. put her on the flight at the lake. Richard met her in Chicago and got her settled in a nursing home with which he was familiar.

She flew on September 10, 2001, the day before 9/11 when every civilian plane in the country would be grounded.

Lillian never really recovered. She talked about seeing Joseph waiting for her. By November, she had gone to be with him. Richard Jr. and his wife, Polly, were instrumental in helping with funeral arrangements. Sterling roses were utilized.

A few months later, Jedi the Golden Retriever became ill during a trip to the lake. It was hopeless. It was his time. Richard and Diane returned to the Chicago condo without their dog. Richard was inconsolable and would barely get out of bed. He felt that without his parents, the showroom, or the dog, that he had no purpose in life. Richard was a sad sight. Diane couldn't bear it.

"Okay," she said, "let's go to the pound and find a dog." Richard had never been able to get dressed so quickly before.

The Chicago dog pound, deep on the south side, was a kill shelter. Death was in the air. Diane felt overwhelmed by the number of cages filled with dogs approved for adoption.

Finally, she said, "I have to have a face I can bond with. I will pick ten faces, then it is up to you, Richard. The dog has to work with your wheelchair."

One beautiful female, tan with a black mask, was overeager and really seemed to plead for attention. Diane put a star by her name. Diane could see the intelligence in this dog. Her eyes insistently followed Diane around the cage.

Richard felt the dog should be female because it would hurt too much to say, "Here boy!" Richard walked several of the dogs with the chair and it boiled down to the starred female and a male. Richard took the female, a thirty-eight pound Rhodesian ridgeback mix puppy with a teddy bear coat. Richard wanted to continue with the *Star Wars* theme begun with Jedi, so he named her Padmé Amidala, Queen of Naboo. Of course she became Paddy, and sometimes Pad.

Richard Jr.'s son visited right after Padmé became part of the family. Richard's namesake loved the dog and played with her at a level that Richard and Diane could not provide. It was clear the boy loved the dog.

As for the elder Richard, he proudly took the dog out and made his rounds past the Oprah studio, and on around to Madison Street. On one such walk, a car stopped suddenly. Glass all black. They wanted to jump Richard for money, but Padmé let out her bark, which was scary indeed, and the car took off.

"Good job, girl, "said Richard. The dog grew to ninety-five pounds and was sweet as could be, but people took one look and were afraid of her. She was a true guard dog.

Diane and Richard now had charge of both lake houses and were spending more and more time in the lake region. With so much space, Diane arranged a Williams family reunion at the lake. Sheryl came with her husband, Aunt Eleanor's son with his wife, and Vernon Williams determined to drive up from Texas even though he was seventy-six years old. Jacob and Kallista brought the kids down from Wisconsin.

It was a special time for Jacob to tap into Harry's family. Jacob carried so many of Harry's traits. Jacob asked Vernon about his grandfather, the grandfather he never knew.

"Well," said Vernon, "he was a lot of fun. Let me tell you about the day my ship arrived at Pearl Harbor …"

69. Hoover Dam
Las Vegas, 2002
James, Jillian

James had felt like Jillian regarded him as a father figure, and she was in her rebellious years. Rather than a serious life partner, he found himself with a child who wanted to go out partying with her young friends all weekend. After he cleared up all her bills, it was time to party. There were lies and cover-ups and finally he had enough. He was tired of being disappointed and angry with her.

At the house, alone, he reflected, America had not really panned out the way he wanted it to pan out. He was seeing somebody else, and had some level of hope for something working out personally for him, but she lived with her mother, who gave men the evil eye. He feared the woman was looking for a port in the storm. There had not been an avenue to develop his own business. His disappointment abounded.

James loved Lake Mead and the Hoover Dam. He went there often to reflect. Despite his love for America and the desert, he felt alone.

70. The Cubs in the Playoffs?
October 2003
Diane and Richard, Sheryl, Sal and Jacob

Only a short time before the playoffs, Diane and Richard relaxed at the lake. Their Chicago condo was on the market. They were too busy trying to manage both lake properties.

For once, the Cubs were playing in October. The entire family were huge Cubs fans, Jacob probably most intensely, although Sal would not agree. Jacob had played baseball. He was quite talented as a left-handed first baseman. Once, within minutes of Diane's arrival in Wisconsin, Jacob scored an unassisted double play at first base.

Sal had called them at the lake to say she had Cubs playoff tickets, in the handicapped section. She invited Diane and Richard to Chicago so they could all go to the playoffs. She had four tickets, two for herself and a friend, two for Diane and Richard. At that time, Jacob and his family were living in Madison, Wisconsin, a bit over two hours from Chicago. Diane just had to offer her ticket to Jacob. Naturally, Jacob accepted.

Diane was happy for this family time. Sal was in a bad accident earlier that year while on the way to have lunch on Diane's birthday. Instead of a leisurely lunch, Diane drove to the accident site hardly able to breathe. She spoke to Sal via cell phone, so she knew Sal was basically okay, but was she injured badly?

Diane was unprepared for the sight of Sal's Volvo convertible crunched to shambles. A driver talking on the phone had come over a hill and rear-ended Sal's car as she was stopped at a light, shoving her convertible under a pickup truck.

After months of therapy, Sal was doing better. Diane was relieved to have some relaxed family time. As usual, she arranged the logistics. She and Jacob would meet near Wrigley Field and Diane would drive Jacob's car back up to Sal's place so he would get to the game in time. Mission accomplished. Diane reclaimed her own car outside Sal's and went home to watch the game on the television. Richard and the girls parked right next to the ballpark in the handicapped section of the parking lot.

The four of them enjoyed a wonderful time. The Cubs lost, but went into overtime with a home run to put them into extra innings. It was really fun, slapping high fives all around through much of the game. Richard had the time of his life. The handicapped section was located behind home plate. Afterwards, on their way out to the handicapped parking, they noticed an Aston Martin parked next to Richard's Buick Riviera. Just then, the owner arrived. It was Michael Jordan. He was very nice to the group and allowed photos. It was a magical night for Sal and Jacob and their stepfather. For a while, they sat in the street outside Sal's house and Richard talked about one of his favorite baseball heroes, a particular hero who was not doing well physically.

"Sometimes, it is just time," said Richard.

Two days later, Richard was back in the hospital with another raging infection. Sal and her friend stopped by, but Richard Jr. had not made it in yet. It was a long way, and he was used to these episodes with his father. Diane looked at the amount of I.V. bags hanging on the stand. They had been cautioned about running out of antibiotics at the lake. Diane was worried. For many years, Richard and Diane had been told that if infection ever hit the heart patch, there would be no recovery. Diane kissed Richard. She had to get back to Padmé in the condo. True to form, Richard was more worried about the dog than about himself.

Diane's cousin, Sheryl, was with her. Sheryl's father, like Vern's father, had been one of Harry's older brothers. Alice had four boys, but the eldest had died after he returned from fighting in WWI. Dennis drowned in the family pond. Sheryl's dad, Don, almost died that day trying to save Dennis. Harry had been only nine years old and had run for help; help which came too late for Dennis. Sheryl had offered to drive up to Chicago from down home to be with Diane. Diane was grateful.

71. A Field of Yellow Roses
Chicago Northwestern Hospital, October 21, 2003
Richard, Diane, Sheryl, Jacob, Richard Jr., Polly, Sal, Jacob

The next day, Diane called Richard to tell him that she and Sheryl were on the way to Northwestern Hospital. "Anything I can bring you, Richard?" Diane asked.

"Yes," he said, "could you bring me up some of the soup you brought yesterday? I really liked that."

"Sure," she said. I have one errand, and then we will be there. Diane wanted to bring him another one of his favorite treats.

Diane and Sheryl arrived at the hospital, bought the soup and made their way upstairs to Richard's room. The nurse explained they were doing a bedside scan. Diane and Sheryl waited with the tray of soup and other treats. The technician backed out of the room and Diane entered.

"The lovely soup is here for you, Richard." Diane said as she walked into the room. Her hands started to shake as she lowered the tray onto the stand. Richard was not right.

"Richard, Richard," she implored. She shook him. Sheryl ran to get the nurse. Richard was completely unresponsive. She knew he was gone. She always knew if he got his chance, he would run for the hills and get out of that chair. The nurse and doctor pulled Diane out of the room; she did not want to go. The room was going to fill up with medical people.

Everything moved in slow motion for Diane. She could not use a cell phone. The nurse at the station barely looked up as she pointed to a pay phone down the hall. Diane's hands were shaking too hard. Sheryl helped her get the coins into the phone slots. The first call was to Richard, Jr. Diane told him the doctors were trying to resuscitate his father.

"This can't be happening." Richard Jr. bolted out the door headed to Chicago, his wife Polly with him. Diane also made a call to Sal, who called Jacob. He, too, bolted out the door toward Chicago.

Richard could not be brought back. By the time Richard Jr. arrived, Diane sat in the room with Richard's body, heartbroken. Her eyes locked with Richard Jr.'s.

"I can't do this," she said. Richard Jr. was inconsolable, but he would be a pillar of strength through the funeral, as was his wife, Sal and Jacob.

Jacob stayed with Diane that night as she sobbed in her room. He gave her wine and tried to hide the wheelchair. Diane finally cried herself to sleep around 4 am. About 6 am, she felt strong hands on her shoulders, as if standing behind her. In a dream state, she clearly heard the words, "You can do this, Diane."

"Richard," she whispered, "Richard …"

Diane set about having a wonderful funeral for Richard where he grew up in Chicago Heights. Richard wanted to be cremated, but his body had been preserved in case Mary and her daughter wanted to see him. Diane worked hard to portray the details of Richard's life, including his fire department uniform. Many members of the fire department came, as well as many friends of Lillian and Joseph. These were the most difficult moments for Diane since Harry died thirty-three years earlier. Bette Midler's *Wind Beneath My Wings* played at the funeral. A live vocalist sang the song at Diane and Richard's wedding.

Diane returned to the condo and Padmé in despair. She just did not want to move and only went out to take the dog for her needs. After a few days, Sal called and asked her to meet for breakfast at the Breakfast Club just outside the West Loop. Diane agreed to a late breakfast. She did not want crowds.

As Diane entered the restaurant, it was empty except for Sal sitting at a table. Each table sported a spray of yellow roses, and she knew it. Her grin was contagious. Diane was so happy to be there with Sal in the field of yellow roses.

Section Four: Snippets 72-81
Finishing the Old (2003-2007)

72. Homecoming
England, October 2003
James

James did not want to go back home again, but he knew he had no choice. He loved America, but America had worn him out. These six years he knew he had not been his regular self in America. It had been about survival, in Las Vegas, and he had chosen women badly. Now, above all, he wanted to spend time with his family. James felt out-of-sorts and, for a period of time, worked at a store selling furniture. Eventually, he bought a flat and reentered the world of public relations and marketing.

He dated a couple of women, but his heart was not in it. He knew one was wild about him, a nurse who had met him at the furniture store, but he just didn't have it in him to extend himself any further. His flat provided a quiet refuge. He would listen to Deep Purple or Styx; maybe a little Pink Floyd, although his taste was quite catholic.

After a few months, he started emailing a few friends and contacts back in the states.

73. The Nursing Home and the Bronze Star
Wisconsin, 2003
Laverne and family

Laverne's family put him in a nursing home prior to his eightieth birthday. Barbara had died. His children were fighting. The house and everything in it was sold, his life pared down to his clothing, his wedding ring, and his Bronze Star. He had done his duty as far as he could, but in the end, Paul had taken over with Barbara and pushed him away. It was not surprising. He was disappointed with life in general, but he looked forward to visits from Janet and her children, Ken and Jill.

He tried to not even think about Diane, a faded illusion now. It had been fourteen years since she called to say she was marrying Richard, and Laverne hoped she would live happily ever after. He had been so proud of the articles about her Chicago Merchandise Mart showroom. She really made a go of it.

Laverne was lonely. He stared out the window, fixed upon a hill in the distance and the forested frosting atop the hill. His Jeep had just been hit in the Hürtgen Forest, just an hour before he posed for the photo. Sometimes he felt life was just a pose.

74. The Miracle of Email
Lake House, 2004
Diane, James, Janet

Diane hid at her lake house well into 2004, although she contracted two major projects in Chicago that would have her driving back and forth for a while. The condo finally sold the following March. Just as it sold, Diane got the call she had been dreading. Lea was gone. Diane flew to the funeral in Wisconsin and took the opportunity to visit Jacob and his family. The memorial to Lea was everything she deserved. Sam asked Diane and Deb, another of Lea and Diane's old friends, to walk in with the family. The pastor asked the family to line up in order of closeness as a relative. Diane looked at her friend Deb and they took their place at the end of the line, happy to be included.

Returning to Chicago, Diane rented a home in Glen Ellyn in order to have a place to stay when she worked on the projects. Padmé was her companion, and on one occasion afforded needed protection. Diane gave Richard Jr. his grandparents' house at the lake. He had always wanted to live there, and moved his family.

Diane took a break and visited California. Richard's best friend was a woman named Patrice, who went by Ping. She lived with her husband and son on Big Bear Mountain. Ping had a kindness in her eyes that was so genuine. Diane had always been able to see why the honest and true Richard found a friend in her.

Diane knew her own sense of loss of Richard was emotionally acute. Before leaving for California, Diane packed her favorite Josh Groban CD, *To Where You Are*. She just could not live without that song right now. She would go to sleep to its beautiful lyrics, wishing she were with Richard. Once she awoke and could feel his presence. The California trip proved relaxing, and Ping was predictably kind, despite her own feelings of loss. Diane also took time to see Richard's aunt in Fallbrook. Aunt Bethany had once peered over Richard's crib.

Diane returned to her lake retreat and at some point in 2004, she received an email from the Englishman, James. He never had the opportunity to visit the showroom at the Mart. It disappeared so soon after their meeting in New Orleans. He was wondering how the two of them were doing. Diane sighed. Another person to inform, even if she did not know him very well.

James had sent sporadic emails, to which she and Richard responded. They liked this guy. Diane explained that it was no longer the two of them. "Richard passed away in 2003."

Diane then found out James had returned to England the same month Richard died. Both were readjusting, but unaware of the other's problems. James was appropriately sympathetic to Diane's situation, but asked if it would be all right to continue to email her on occasion. She agreed.

During her travels and musings, Diane realized she had not heard from Janet since she ignored the party invitation back in 1997. She wondered how Laverne was doing. Diane could not find Laverne, and struggled to remember Janet's new last name. Finally, through diligent searching on the internet, she found Janet and was able to connect to her. She found out Laverne was still alive in a nursing home. Diane did not realize Laverne was a widower.

75. Jacob's *Valued Possession* Letter

Carlson School of Business, Minneapolis, 2005
Jacob and Kallista, Diane

Jacob's MBA program included two weeks of study in Europe. Just before he and Kallista boarded their international flight, he accepted a position with a major software company. It was big news, but he did not have a chance to tell his parents. Well, Diane planned to join them the last three days in Paris. He could announce the news to her there.

As part of his program, Jacob was required to write a paper on one of his most valued possessions. When Richard died, Jacob asked Diane if he could have Richard's chess set. That was all he wanted, as the two of them had played chess together. Diane did not play and was all too happy for Jacob to have the chess set.

University of Minnesota, Carlson School of Management
September 2005

Valued Possession, by Jacob M.

The Item

This item is a chess set made of pewter, wood and metal. The set is designed in a sort of middle-earth style. It was a relatively expensive set and not particularly in a design or style that I would have chosen had I bought it myself. The set resides in my office and is used sparingly, mostly to educate my young children about the game or to play the occasional guest who notices that I play.

History

This set was purchased by my step-father circa 1990. He was interested in wizards, witches, and dragons and the style was a logical choice for him. Over the years, my step-father and I had many battles on the board, but the smallest part of the significance is the remembrance of those games, there is a much deeper significance.

My step-father was paralyzed from the mid-chest down in a 1983 automobile accident. At the time, he was a successful computer consultant and a lieutenant in the Matteson, Illinois volunteer fire department. He played college football at Purdue and was still a very active middle-aged man.

His struggles from that day were many, not only physical but mental. He had to recreate the way he lived his life. He had to trade a lot of his physical activities for activities of the mind. He had to retrain his attitudes to not take anything for granted. I have the utmost respect for his perseverance, his determination and the adaptation he made. In the many, many years I knew Richard, I never heard him complain about his paralysis. And while sometimes noticeably bothered by his condition, he never let it rule him and maintained a tremendous amount of independence.

How I Obtained It

My step-dad and I went to Game 1 of the 2003 Chicago Cubs vs. Florida Marlins National League championship Series at Wrigley Field in Chicago. He had not been feeling real well, but the Cubs were another curse that we both shared. After the game (a loss of course) we went to the handicapped/reserved parking lot and found we were parked next to Michael Jordan's Aston Martin. We had a short conversation with Michael and got a few pictures snapped. My step-dad then dropped me off at my sister's and then I motored on home. I had a Financial Accounting exam in two nights and had to get back. You always think there is going to be another perfect night right around the corner, or in this case an almost perfect night. However, my step-father passed away just five days later. The cause: his body went toxic from all the infections he had dealt with over the years, the direct cause: his 1983 automobile accident.

What followed was a whirlwind of family difficulties. My mother wanted me to take anything of Richard's that I thought I would want. I only wanted one thing, it is one thing that we not only shared, but to me represented what my step-father was more than anything else. That of course was his pewter chess set from middle earth.

Evolution

The set's evolution has been somewhat unique. It started out as a chess set that was not that practical, it is sometimes difficult to ascertain between black and white pieces. It is in a style that I am not particularly fond of, or at least does not fit my personality.

The set's value is probably $200 new in a game store. This in itself is a significant amount for a man that never like to spend money on anything. The big reason it is so important to me is it was important to him based on the amount he spent on it, the games we played, and its representation of the life he lived. It is an ongoing representation of my step-father and the good qualities that he exuded to me in our relationship. Now the set is priceless to me.

*** *

Diane had always dreamed of seeing Paris and recently purchased a numbered and signed serigraph of Kondakova's *Autumn on the Seine*. Now she had an opportunity to meet family there. Diane flew to Paris alone in the spring, able to speak only a few words in French. Jacob and Kallista spent most of the two-week study program in Lyon then traveled by train to Paris.

Diane arrived early on her first trip to Europe, to rest up for Paris. She thought of Normandy, of Laverne, and her uncle Dall Roth who died in the war. She never knew him.

Paris was everything Diane had ever hoped. "If only I could have shared it with Richard," she thought to herself. Then her mind wandered back to Laverne. She closed her eyes and imagined them together as they had been twenty years before. Paris would have been made for them. They were so alive together. Diane resolved to check in on him with Janet when she returned.

Jacob made his new job announcement and Diane was ecstatic. She took Jacob and Kallista to a wonderful celebration dinner. The French Onion soup was echelons above any American version. Diane went on and on about it until Kallista had to order some.

Jacob went off with another man in the program to see Normandy; Jacob was a WWII buff. He was very emotional upon his return. Diane knew Normandy had stilled his heart. Meanwhile, in a more frivolous mood, Kallista and Diane enjoyed the Champs Elysées[9].

Over the three days, they did all the usual tourist meanderings, although Diane preferred to sit at the Seine alone rather than go through the Notre Dame Cathedral. She had been unprepared for how much Europe made her think about Laverne and what different circumstances had brought him to Europe as a young man.

That night, Diane dreamed of Laverne, both of them twenty years younger, in Paris, in love. The dream was vivid and Diane felt an enormous sense of freedom in the dream, a freedom she had never experienced in life. She awoke with a start and felt as if Laverne was in the room with her.

---

[9] The street Elysian Fields in New Orleans was named for this famous French boulevard. "What a difference between the two," Diane thought. Elysian Fields, except near the French Quarter, was poverty row.

76. Facing the Past
Lake House, 2005
Diane, Janet, Laverne, Magna

Upon her return from France, Diane found messages from Janet. Diane was spent, but she read them intently. First, the loss of Richard, and now to hear Laverne was in poor health and alone. Details about him had not come easily from Janet, but now Diane was getting the full picture. Of course, Janet knew nothing of the past, so she gave few details about Laverne. Janet simply thought he was Diane's ex-boss. Even spent, Diane wanted to take care of Laverne at her lake house. That meant explaining everything to Janet about the past. Perhaps it was time. Diane responded to Janet in an email.

Dear Janet,

I have been so happy to reconnect with you - even though it brought the sadness of knowing your dad is alone and not well. Janet, I woke up this morning knowing that today was the day that you should be told certain things about the past. Recently you told me that you are estranged from your brother - and of course, your mother is gone. As an only child, I can appreciate those feelings.

Call me crazy, but I awoke with a vivid dream this morning that has sent me to the computer to write to you today. You can choose your way to confirm this with your father; please do not upset him. This is difficult for me, and yet, I believe it is time. You may not be happy with me at first, but I pray that you read this letter through and see in it the truth and love that only time and hindsight can bear out. I have always liked and respected you, and well ... you are so much like your dad.

Back in 1979, I became painfully aware that my husband was cheating on me. I had indisputable proof. One day (very unprofessionally), I broke down at work. You might think your dad would have none of that nonsense in his showroom, but that's not what happened. He told me my husband must be crazy, and that he (Laverne) had been in love with me for a long time. He said he knew it was silly because of the age difference, but he could not keep it to himself any longer. For me, a woman who had been ridiculed at home, he was like the oasis in the desert. At the time, I thought perhaps my own feelings were just rebound, but I came to know better. I loved your father with all my heart and soul. When Steve finally came to me with the truth and asked for a divorce, your father asked me to marry him.

In the end, I could not do it. There was not only the age difference - but far more importantly - there were more people to hurt than my already hurting children. I could not do to another family what had been done to mine, and I do not believe he would have been happy that way either. I had children to raise and he needed to be Grandpa. I asked him not to short change your mother - I have no idea how he did with that. And so ... a friend asked me to come to Chicago, and I felt I could not stay in Wisconsin - with a whole school system whispering about me - and the situation with your dad, I just had to leave and start over. I was also closer to family there. I did not know at the time that I could not have custody of my children if I left Wisconsin. Financially, I needed the job I found in Chicago, so the kids were raised with joint custody and Jacob spent the school year with his dad in Wisconsin, summers and holidays with us in Chicago. It worked out.

In the late 1990s, I received your invitation to Laverne and Barbara's 50th wedding anniversary. I threw it away. I guess I always imagined that Laverne's family went blissfully forward, but your recent comments seem to indicate some trouble. It pains me terribly that your dad is sick and alone in a home. I pray that you forgive me for getting involved with your father so long ago. I was not strong then. I was young and alone and very much in need of his love and caring. He was not an easy man to say 'no' to. My faith seemed to evaporate - yet, his seemed to grow stronger.

I pray that you read this with the wisdom that age and time bring us all. I had to tell you - I cannot be your friend at this time unless you *know the truth. I cannot ask to have Laverne with me unless you understand the past, and indeed I am asking for that. I have spent much time in hospitals and with visiting nurse practitioners. I have learned much from them. Let's talk.*

Blessings to you and yours, Diane

Diane hit the send button and almost immediately, a reply email from Janet came back.

Dear Diane,

When I saw the subject line of your e-mail, I had to stop what I was doing and open your letter.

I don't have time now to fully respond to you, but I can imagine that you are anxious about that response, so I wanted to quickly get word back to you not to worry, and I am not upset with you in the least.

I am thrilled that you shared this information about my dad with me. I have shared with my husband but will not say anything to the kids just now. I am grateful to you for being close to my dad. I always knew he cared about you and was so proud of your career, but of course, I didn't really know! More another time. Janet

Diane again asked if she might take care of Laverne at her lake house. Janet would be welcome anytime. Diane explained all she had learned from Richard's nurses. She felt confident that she could handle most circumstances.

Janet struggled, but in the end, after telling Laverne that Diane wanted him and seeing him light up like a Christmas tree, she agreed to transport Laverne to Chicago. Diane would meet them. Diane had not seen Laverne for seventeen years, and she prepared herself for an old man. It would be workable. Laverne was the great passion of her life. She had loved Richard with all she had – he was the most honest man she knew – but nobody had ever compared to the romance that was Laverne in her mind. Nobody. The dynamics would be different. She was the strong one now, spent or not. She would take him to the lake house to relax.

He sat in the passenger seat, giving Diane the smile of a lifetime. He was happy, she could see. She didn't want to tax him, so she had made hotel reservations in Chicago and then again near her Aunt Magna's en route to the lake region. Aunt Magna was not doing well and Diane took every opportunity to see her. Laverne would understand.

He hugged her and kissed her on the neck. Janet busied herself with unloading most of his belongings into Diane's car so the former lovers could have a couple of minutes with each other. Diane felt tears erupting. Laverne laughed. "Crying again are we?" The two women got him settled in the hotel room and they all had coffee, his with cream, of course. Diane felt nervous and warm all at the same time.

Janet had a tough work schedule and was starting back to Wisconsin almost immediately. It wasn't long until Diane and Laverne were alone. In some ways, it was as if no time had passed.

"I hope you aren't expecting me to be much of a Romeo," Laverne said. Diane realized he might not know Richard was a paraplegic. She would save that conversation for later.

"I really wasn't worried about all that, Laverne. I just want to be with you. We can finally be together anytime we would like to. Isn't that fun?" She tried to keep it upbeat for him.

Janet had cautioned Diane not to let him make any attempts at sex. "It could be deadly."

Privately, Diane hoped the years had changed things so that she could manage Janet's request.

"I am very tired," he said. She helped him to get undressed and into bed. He was soon asleep. She let him sleep. They could order room service anytime.

Morning was beautiful. It took Laverne a minute to realize where he was and who he was with. Diane was so happy just to be with him. She already felt comfortable. His morning routine was considerably easier to deal with than Richard's was, even though Richard had been so independent. They had breakfast in the room and then took off to the south.

"I do have one stop to make, Laverne," she said, "before we stay at the next hotel. My dear Aunt Magna is not well in a nursing home and I fear she won't live much longer."

Magna. Laverne thought about that name. Dall's wife was named Magna. Wheels turned. Magna was not an everyday name. "What is your aunt's last name, Diane?"

"Schroeder. Her husband was a Methodist minister."

"I see," said Laverne. "A guy with me in the war had a wife named Magna, and they were from Illinois, but his last name was Roth."

Diane hit the brakes and pulled to the side of the road. "You were in the war with my Uncle Dall Roth? The uncle I never knew?" Diane could feel her chest heaving, tears welling up. She could not breathe properly.

"Yes!" Laverne was quiet for a minute, then he said, "He was my best friend over there, but he was killed in an instant on the Bridge. I could not help him."

That damn bridge again.

Diane was stunned. Why had they not known this before? Of course, Ione always told Diane that Dall died in the Battle of the Bulge. She had never equated Dall with Laverne's bridge. Now thoughts pulled backwards to Laverne's earlier stories. The Bridge at Remagen. Laverne earned his Bronze Star there. Diane began to remember the story. Years had passed since they discussed The Bridge. In earlier days, Laverne would advise Diane if the movie about the bridge was going to be on television. He wanted her to watch it.

"Will I be able to talk to Magna?" Laverne looked at once concerned and seemed agitated. Diane worried these war memories were too much. "Yes, of course," she said.

The Bridge flashed through Laverne's mind. He could see Dall's lifeless face as clearly as on the day he died, the day that ended with Laverne soaked in blood. The memories were tough, but he found himself excited to meet Magna, the beautiful woman in Dall's photos.

Diane got a wheelchair for Laverne. It was a long walk to Magna's room and she did not want him to be exhausted. She was well-acquainted with wheelchair logistics and made things easy for him. Diane had seen Magna only two weeks earlier and had feared she would not see her again. Magna was ninety-five years old. Diane introduced Laverne as a friend, her ex-boss from Wisconsin. Magna was weak, but she acknowledged. Diane didn't want to cause her any pain, but she thought she knew her aunt well enough that she would want to talk to somebody who was with Dall in the end.

Diane helped Laverne from the chair and he walked over to the bedside. "Magna, hello. I used to see your photo every day while we were in Germany. Dall was my best friend over there. We were on the bridge together."

"My God," she murmured. Then she said, "I've aged." All three laughed.

"Did you see him die?" Aunt Magna looked like the world's wisdom lived in her eyes.

"He died instantly, Magna. He did not suffer. He was one of the bravest going out onto that bridge that day under fire."

Then Laverne showed her the Bronze Star in his pocket.

The room went silent, then Magna said, "Thank you for doing this, Diane. Thank you for bringing more peace to your old aunt." Diane had wondered how Magna and Laverne could handle this. The room was emotionally heavy. They were superstars.

No more talk was necessary between Laverne and Magna. All love and truth drifted as a cloud in the air. Magna was exhausted. Soon, Diane and Laverne were on their way.

Laverne and Diane drove on. It had been quite an experience. Laverne looked at Diane. "Your dad was the Harry who wrote Dall letters, wasn't he?"

"Yes, Laverne, he was," said Diane. "And I have some of those letters at the lake. You can read them while we are there."

No sooner had Laverne settled at the lake than Hurricane Katrina hit New Orleans. Sal had moved back only a few months earlier. She abandoned her house, drove north on the contraflow lanes of I-55 with her animals, two beagles named Jambalaya and Olive, and two cats named Kokoro and Galileo. She also had another human being in the car and precious little else. Sal was smart and had remembered her insurance paperwork. She stopped a while at the lake, then pressed on to Chicago to her friend's house, where she and the animals would be well-tended. When the levees broke, both Sal and Diane feared the worst for Sal's house.

77. Look-and-Leave
New Orleans, 2005
Sal and Diane

Officials announced in early October, that Sal's neighborhood in New Orleans would be open just for a look-and-leave. Sal was despondent. The internet news was not good for her neighborhood. The race track to the north of Sal had been deeply under water. Yet, she was close to the Esplanade Ridge, and her home sat about halfway from the French Quarter to City Park, the French Quarter being high ground in this case, up against the Mississippi River levees. City Park flooded near Lake Pontchartrain to the north, the location of one of the levee breaks. The Federal government, specifically the Army Corps of Engineers, controlled the levees, not the city of New Orleans.

Diane had immediately booked flights for Sal and herself. Janet stayed with Laverne while Diane flew with her daughter to their favorite city, New Orleans. They landed to hurrahs and shouts from the flight crew, picked up a rental car and headed into the city, mouths agape at what they saw.

Devastation everywhere. They had huge lumps in their throats, filtered masks and bottled water packed in their suitcases. When they saw City Park and the beautiful Live Oaks and Bald Cypress on the ground, they both started crying. Sal's house was only blocks away. They headed down the Esplanade. The neighborhood looked like army-occupied Germany must have after the war, a city under military rule.

As Sal and Diane pulled up to the house, they noted the beautiful shutters lying on the ground. At least they are here, Diane thought. "Sal," she said, "the waterline is just a bit above your door. Could it be that all was not lost?" Sal unlocked her front door and walked in. Cherry bookcases lined the front room filled with books, some of them rare. Diane had the bookcases made up during the showroom years. Mississippi silt covered the original cypress floors, but there was no sign of the mold they had expected. Floodwater had encroached about three inches. Officials told them the water receded an inch a day, and the house had been wet approximately three to four days. After six weeks away from home, Sal wept for joy. Her book collection was intact, art work hung on the walls. The house had been built in the 1860s. Perhaps it was a tough old house after all. Her family photographs were untouched. Sal had not been the victim of flood nor of foul play.

Sal had made arrangements to stay with friends in the French Quarter, as the look-and-leave lasted twenty-four hours only.

But Diane knew her daughter. "You want to sleep in your own bed, don't you?"

Sal did. They checked out the guest room and Sal asked her mother if she minded sleeping in a room with window panes blown out. Diane did not. They cleaned up the glass and started on the silt. Cleaning the refrigerator consumed much of the day. It was one of the most disgusting things Diane had ever seen.

"Only your mother would clean this with you," said Sal, and Diane believed she was right. Of course, in the end, it would be replaced and wind up on the curb like most of the refrigerators in New Orleans. They went to the only fast food place they could find open. There was a sign outside that said, "This is what you are having."

The women returned to Illinois after the look-and-leave, but two weeks later, Sal, impatient with waiting for her home, returned home to New Orleans without full utilities. The cats stayed in Chicago, but the two dogs returned with her. She brought her friend's large dog back with her as well for protection. Her dear friend was nursing a bad ankle and could more easily take care of cats. Sal felt much better with a large dog and a total of three dogs in the house. Most of her neighbors were still gone. Miraculously, FEDEX was operating. Diane sent Sal urgent clothes pins and tuna packets, as she had no refrigeration and there wasn't an available clothes pin in New Orleans. Sal had electricity. She could wash clothes, but the gas was off. She could not cook or dry clothes. Sal lost weight, and true to form, felt she should help others not as fortunate as she. She was to see things far worse than the refrigerator.

Diane worried about Sal, but slowly Sal's friends returned. One friend was a counselor for the Coast Guard, who kept counseling, even though her own home was moldy to the ceiling and her only son was serving in the middle-east. The Coast Guard had put her in a hotel. Sal was a tiger working with her insurance companies, and soon repairs began on her house. The years working in the housing industry paid off. Sal knew just what to do.

78. Magna's Funeral
Lake House and Chicago, 2006
Diane, Laverne, James

Diane regretted she and Laverne never had the opportunity to run a business of their own. His savvy and her talent would have turned the world golden. But it was enough, she thought, just to spend these days together with no obligations except to each other. He was, after all, her one great love and precious minutes now ticked sweetly through each day. She thought about the day so long ago when he had told her to watch her efficiency – she had only worked for him a few weeks at the time – in the most military fashion. She smiled into her morning coffee. Laverne was reading Dall and Harry's letters again. He loved to read them over and over.

Diane was about the same age now as Laverne was when they first become involved and fell in love. She thought about how passionate he had been then and was amazed. That was not possible any longer, but he could still look at her in the most erotic way possible. It is just the way it was between them. He told her now there had been no others after her. He had done his duty and been with Barbara to the end. Diane had always imagined that his family went happily on after she and Laverne bravely ended their relationship, but Janet had informed her such happiness was not the case. Diane would make sure Laverne was happy now.

Diane had more emails from James in England. He was fascinated with the story of Laverne and understood why she wanted to take care of him. James' father had been a *Desert Rat*, part of Britain's 8th Army in World War II. James was a writer and a romantic. Diane had learned that much about him. He talked about coming to America and wanted to visit her and Laverne. Diane wasn't sure about that. She thought the Englishman was becoming fond of her and she didn't want Laverne to see that.

Janet was on call. She would fly to be with Laverne as soon as Diane got word of Magna's death. As fate would have it, James' flight into Chicago coincided with Magna's funeral. Diane would be able to meet him before returning to Laverne. She had not seen the Englishman in person for several years, but he had shared photos.

Magna's funeral was glorious. Methodist ministers came together to see her off, and her family, the children she'd raised, did a beautiful job. Her youngest girl, Jen, traveled from California and gave the main eulogy. Diane embraced her afterwards. Jen had named her daughter after Diane because of their sweet times together in earlier years. Those sweet times at Magna's home and the fried chicken … Diane had been told many times that Magna was at the hospital the day she almost died as a baby … she could just picture that pillar of strength being there for Harry and Ione. Magna outlived them both. Except for the youngest of Magna's seven siblings, Magna had buried them all. Certainly, that day the heavens opened to receive her, certainly.

There was a reception in the church basement in the little town of Weldon, Illinois. Diane had driven past Magna's old house with the chime she loved. It looked so small. Diane had thought to bring Harry's letters to Aunt Magna and Uncle Dall because there might be some Roth relatives at the funeral. Indeed, Glenn Roth was there and was quite moved that Diane had brought the letters. His daughter, Celena, and her husband Dan also were engrossed in the letters. Celena and Diane exchanged address information and vowed to stay in touch. Glenn was so happy to spend time with somebody who had any remembrance of his brave older brother, Dall. Glenn thought about the bridge, but did not mention it to Diane. Diane decided the story of Laverne was too long to tell at the reception, and she wanted to keep the focus on Dall for his relatives.

Diane drove her rental car back to Chicago and checked in late at her hotel. She was to meet James the next day and she was exhausted and drained. She would chat with him, but soon catch a flight back to the lake and Laverne. Janet was doing fine with Laverne, but she would need to get back to work.

James looked like a breath of fresh air. He was alive, handsome, and vibrant. She knew he was five years her junior. Perhaps taking care of people and burying them had taken its toll; perhaps she was too familiar now with the world of the elderly, but he took her breath away. Maybe for a few minutes she would allow herself to feel young again. James was artistic and musical, theatrical. He loved architecture. He had wanted to be an architect when he was young.

Really, a kindred spirit for her. They both realized it, and laughed about both being left-handed. He told her she was a good woman to take care of Laverne the way she was, especially after everything that had happened with Richard.

"He is not well," she admitted. "I will do it as long as I can and pray that is long enough. I owe him everything, my career, my self-esteem. If it had not been for him, my daughter and I would have starved the first year in Chicago. He is the great love of my life."

"You will have plenty of life left after this, Diane," James reminded gently.

"I can't even go there now, James."

They parted and promised to keep up the emails. There was definitely a spark between them and she knew he wasn't going away anytime soon. Diane raced to the airport. She hated being gone from the lake just now.

Janet looked worried when Diane arrived back at the lake. She, too, had seen the decline. Laverne was sleeping and they talked medical strategy. Diane sought Janet's advice and approval on everything.

79. Bling and Thoughts
Christmas Week, 2006
Diane and Laverne

Laverne's eyes sparkled as Diane put up the Christmas tree. It was difficult for her, pulling out Richard's precious glass ornaments from Marshall Fields. As a young man, Richard the Purdue linebacker had fought off crowds of women after Christmas to purchase those ornaments. She smiled and felt sorry for the women who might have been in the way of that massive football-trained chest and arms. Diane felt she was about to lose another love, and she intended to make this the best Christmas ever for Laverne. She added more lights to the tree. She wanted it to be full of bling. Diane felt his eyes on her. He never failed to make her feel like a woman, even now. The entirety of their relationship was in every look. Diane soaked in his admiration as if it were water in a desert. She was oblivious of the cold, which was unlike her. The moonlight danced off the lake that night, and for a while, they sat enjoying both the lake view and the tree with the room lights turned off. His eyes were closed.

Laverne had loved Diane for more than twenty-five years, even throughout all those long years apart, years Diane devoted to Richard and her family, years he tried, unsuccessfully, to make Barbara happy. She had never been happy with him, he now realized. It had never been right. It had been something he thought was right from the distance of a German forest. But he did not regret the years with his daughter, Janet, and her children Ken and Jill. If it meant sleeping alone in the basement for decades, so be it. Barbara had been more than happy with her son, a relationship Laverne had found quite odd actually. His mind wandered back to Erika, and he wondered what had become of the baby. Erika had been beautiful; somebody would have married her and raised the child, surely. It was sixty years since he left Germany.

A few weeks later, on January 17th, Laverne celebrated his eighty-third birthday; Diane doubted he would live to see eighty-four. He thanked her often. He was so happy. It reminded her of how Richard had thanked her for performing nursing duties only three or four years earlier.

She finally told Richard, "You would do it for me also."

Richard replied, "If I didn't, I should be shot."

Laverne still had his Bronze Star with him, his most valued possession. He made it clear, however, that it was to go to Janet. Ken already had the luger, Jill some of her grandmother's jewelry. Diane still had the necklace in her jewelry chest, the two entwined gold hearts. Sometimes she wore it around the house just to make Laverne happy. Diane wondered if they had done the right thing in not marrying so long ago. Diane found it ironic that Laverne had outlived Richard. She knew this would be a double-whammy, a twice-widowed feeling, but it was all about him for her … just giving him the happiness a decorated war hero deserved; he was a man of deep emotion who was not afraid to express himself. He put his arms around her every morning and she was extremely comfortable there.

"Diane," he said, "I am so happy to end my years with you. You have no idea. You were a distant memory, and now we are together again. I can't believe how lucky I am. I can look at you anytime I want to and not watch you walk away another time."

"I'm sorry in many ways that I ever left you, Laverne, although I was so happy to be there for Richard as well. And you saw Barbara to the end. I am sure she was happy you never left her."

"I hope so, Diane. She would have been happier with a different man, but that's all water under the bridge now."

"We have this right now, Laverne," Diane smiled. "We have it all right now in this moment."

Diane considered this WWII generation. Harry always told her service to others meant everything. If Harry had lived to retirement, he would have probably driven a bus to take children to church or handed out fruit baskets to the needy on Sunday; that's how he would have spent his time. They certainly knew how to sacrifice. She could not do enough for Laverne. He was her heart and soul. Yet the episodes with Richard and Laverne were taking their toll.

Diane looked in the mirror. She was almost fifty-seven. Time was getting away from her.

Diane still received emails from James, and he was still her private breath of fresh air. He worked at a public relations firm in England and would tell her stories about the company. Somehow, she still felt a part of the business world by reading them. She knew he admired her at a minimum, probably more, but he knew what the situation at the lake was all about. Diane wanted to be there for Laverne as long as he needed her. Sometimes Laverne would tell her she should not be taking care of him.

"You should be out dating."

Diane would laughingly say, "That did not work out that well the first time."

Diane still found herself grieving for Richard, let alone Laverne's impending death on top of it. It was good she had shouldered more than her share over the years, which gave her backbone now. When Laverne held her in his arms in the morning, she could still feel all the original passion. She remembered vividly what their love-making had been like, how compatible they had been in that department. It was enough to lie in his arms and remember. She would often have dreams of Richard, and he would be walking or running in the dreams. In one dream, Jedi the dog was running away from him and Richard was exasperated with him. For a few months more, Diane lived in this dreamland between Richard and Laverne, often living in the past.

Padmé, the Rhodesian ridgeback mix, stood guard.

80. The End of a Long, Long Road
Lake House, April 2007
Laverne and those who loved him

By April, Janet had visited twice and was ever more concerned. Her children, Jill and Ken had visited as well. Diane knew it was odd for them to see their grandfather with her, yet they were gracious. Janet had prepared them well. Laverne's son never showed up, and Diane was not surprised. He sold Laverne's house, took his mother to look after her, and stuck Laverne in a home without telling Janet what was going on. He did not even spring Laverne for Barbara's funeral.

Laverne told Diane he just went along with it. He didn't feel well and was so disappointed at how life had turned out. Well, he was happy now, and that was all Diane cared about at present. Janet was thrilled to see her father happy for a change, but she knew it would not last long. She had been shocked, yet relieved, to find out how long he had loved Diane. It made sense to her, knowing her parents as she did. She had always known how proud Laverne was of Diane after she left Wisconsin, but Janet had never thought it beyond admiration. She just didn't know; never realized the truth. Now she knew why Laverne would not employ a woman other than herself. It was a promise he had made.

Diane had been professionally frustrated without Laverne, as well as personally. She and Laverne had just conducted business without complaint, and definitely no whining. They were both self-starters who did not require help or supervision. As an employer, Diane found that type of person to be very rare indeed. Diane, who did not suffer fools gladly, was certainly surrounded by quite a few of them.

"Yikes," she thought one morning, "how wonderful it is now to just deal with Laverne, who would require, in reality, less babysitting than most people."

Laverne still winked at her; he knew it got her right in the heart, so he kept doing it. She had brought him a cup of coffee in bed, with cream. He winked, and she went back to the kitchen to make some toast. By the time she returned, the stroke had occurred. Diane called 911, but she knew he was gone, just as she had known Richard was gone, just as she had known Ione was gone. As Diane waited for the emergency crew to arrive, sobs wracked her soul again. She put her head on his chest, but she knew he was gone. He had instructed her, made her promise, not to try CPR on him personally. Diane would leave that final decision for the paramedics.

Diane called Janet prior to her departure to the hospital. She told Janet she was quite sure Laverne was gone; he had been transported, but there had been no sign of life. Janet's husband took the phone, as Janet was unable to continue. He was quite helpful in the days to come and the arrangements that had to be made to transport Laverne's body back to Wisconsin. They buried him next to Barbara, but Diane said her good byes at the lake. Jacob stood in for Diane in Wisconsin. Janet had been his Sunday school teacher, and she welcomed him and commented on his beautiful eyes. Jacob had inherited Ione's coloring; he tanned easily, and he had passed these traits on to his eldest daughter, Alexandra. Finally, Ione's characteristics had shown up. Diane often saw herself in Karlin, who had been born on Ione's birthday. Karlin sported her mother's beautiful blue eyes and both girls were as stunning as their mother.

81. The Luger
Wisconsin, May 2007
Ken

Ken turned over the German luger in his hand as tears rolled down his face. He had gone to the lake house to say goodbye to his Grandpa Laverne, but the reality was still something else. His mother, Janet, had broken the news gently to him and to his older sister, Jill. She called Laverne "Grandpa Cough" because Laverne had never conquered the cigarettes. Jill and Ken had been everything to him. Ken remembered how his grandfather had been the one to encourage him in his passion for radio, how he wore crazy clothes to the Indy 500 every year. Ken had spoken to Diane, and now he understood how much his grandfather sacrificed to be around for Ken and his sister. He put the gun away. It made him feel too close to the pain of the battlefield. Someday soon he would bring it out again.

Section Five: Snippets 82-100
Starting Anew (2007-2014)

82. Alive again
England, 2007
James and Diane

James gave Diane a few months to grieve, then invited her to England, insisted really. Amazingly, Diane was ready. She had spent the summer in recovery. Reading and swimming were her activities. She went to New Orleans to see Sal and let herself languish in the healing balm of the French Quarter. The Vieux Carré never failed her. She discovered new cafés in the Marigny and walked early mornings in City Park, usually near the arched bridge to the Pavilions. The Spanish moss shaded the morning and was a cool treat, even in the heat of the New Orleans summer. Diane loved the silver color of the moss and felt transported just looking at it. By the end of summer, she allowed herself to think about the rest of her life. Diane planned a September trip to England.

James met her at Heathrow Airport, and they soon sped north along the M40. Diane gasped at the patchwork quilt of fields in the panorama as they sped over the first hill. She would return in May, and the quilt would be filled with bright gold squares, different from any field in Iowa. The golden color took her breath away.

Diane's family had come from England in the 17th Century, sailing on the ship *The Planter* from London. Her ancestors, the Tingleys, came from Surrey.[10] At that moment, there was something

---

[10] Palmer Tingley (or Tingle), a miller aged twenty-one, boarded The Planter on April 8, 1635, a few days before sailing. The ship arrived in Boston, Massachusetts Bay Colony on June 7, 1635. He came with a certificate that indicated his origins, "being from the minister of Kingston upon Thames in the County of Surrey". After his arrival, he married Anna (Hannah) Fosdick in Charlestown, Massachusetts; they had a son, Samuel. Palmer fought in the Pequot War and was thus awarded eight acres of land in Ipswich, Massachusetts, where he settled in 1639. He died shortly thereafter, leaving the one son. Anna remarried and had seven more children with James Barrett. From the Tingley lineage came Governor Clyde Tingley of New Mexico, the Carrie Tingley Hospital, Albuquerque, and The Tingley Coliseum, Albuquerque; in addition, the Tingley Memorial Library, Bradenton Beach, Florida, by benefactor Beulah Hooks Hannah Tingley. Beulah was a 1944 delegate to the Democratic National Convention in Chicago. In 1953, she married Harvey

distinctly like new life stirring at her center, yet it really was the realization that this is where her people came from, the Homeland. Diane was, as far as she knew, one hundred percent British in descent. Harry's name was Welsh, and Alice had been Irish. Ione's people, Frank Craig's ancestors, sailed from London to America. Ione's mother had been of Scottish descent.

James and Diane knew each other fairly well at this point, thanks to the internet, plus the age old telephone. They were fairly certain they had first encountered back in 1982 at the Marshall Field's cosmetic counter, and she was still enamored of his accent, of course. But it was more than that. Diane admired men who did not butcher the English language, and this writer certainly did not, one of many necessary characteristics for Diane. He wore his black hair combed back in an Italian style, and he greeted her in a suit and tie. He was grinning from ear to ear in his exuberant style. He described himself as, "basically shy," yet James was the first to shake hands with people. "Compensation," he called it.

James lived in a flat in a converted factory building. The entrance to the car park looked like a small version of the Tower Bridge, very cute and quaint, Diane thought. She was comfortable enough to stay with him. He offered to sleep in the second bedroom.

At fifty-seven and exhausted from travel, Diane took him up on that offer in order to refresh herself and catch her breath. "Besides," she told herself, "this guy has been hanging out with women much younger." Diane wanted to take a temperature reading in the light of day, after she was rested.

James found the second bedroom uncomfortable and hoped the sleeping arrangement might change. Diane did look more relaxed than when he had seen her in Chicago, but she had just come from her Aunt's funeral then and was headed back to Laverne. Diane knew his history. She knew about the young woman in Las Vegas as well as the one he had dated in England. James felt himself ready for a woman of substance, and he was sure Diane was that woman. He had his fill of bad women, or his bad choices, whichever. His mother Joanne was very strong and the family had always leaned on her. Joanne liked being in charge and could run the country, but she

---

Ellsworth Tingley of Bradenton Beach, Florida. (From the Tingley-United website and other sources).

174

had no guile in her. James wanted a strong woman who had no guile in her. That's what he wanted. Diane was classy, knew her way around business and art. He knew he was already in love with her. But was Diane ready for that?

The next morning, James heard her in the loo and readied a tray of tea and toast.

"Tea is on the table if you are ready," he raised his voice so she would hear. Diane appeared in her silk robe, hair combed, looking fresh without makeup. "I knew she didn't need any in 1982," he thought. She still didn't. She looked younger than her years, even after all she had been through.

"Good skin genes," she once said, inherited from her mother Ione.

Diane surveyed the Englishman. He seemed eager to please her. There it was, that breath of fresh air. Diane did not kid herself; she had sensed damage in this man. Unavoidable, most likely, at their ages. She wondered how deep the damage ran. They knew each other well at this point. They'd thoroughly discussed everything from religion to politics and often shared viewpoints. Diane had found many American men her age just too conservative for her tastes. The Englishman was worldlier, definitely continental and sported a larger world view than most of the men she knew back in America. He often used phrases that Diane had not heard since Harry used them, which warmed her heart.

James showed her as much as he could about his history that day, but they did not go around to his parents' home yet. They walked the canals. Diane marveled at the very old buildings and the new modern structures that reminded her of Chicago. The narrowboats fascinated her. They bought coffee at one such boat. Diane had been to Paris, but this was her first time in England. She felt the culture shock, certainly, but her eyes were for the tall athletic Englishman with the expressive brown eyes. He showed her his holy ground, the Birmingham City Football Club home stadium. He had played in their junior team and promised to take her to a soccer match while she was there. By the end of the day, Diane was comfortable with him. It was time he moved back into his own bedroom, she thought. It had been about twenty-five years since their supposed encounter in Marshall Fields, and nearly eight years since they met again in New Orleans. Diane smiled at that thought.

James had planned a week away at the seaside in Torquay. For some reason, he wanted to take her there before they visited London. James was not especially fond of going to London, but he would for her, of course. But at the moment, it was time to meet his parents, Joanne and Alfred.

Diane knew James' father Alfred was quite a bit older than Joanne. Alfred had been a *Desert Rat* in WWII, and discovered Joanne some years after the war. They had been together for more than fifty years.

Diane felt immediately comfortable in Joanne and Alfred's home, as if she had always belonged. The cultural comfort hit Diane like a ton of bricks, another one of Harry's sayings. She immediately realized she never fit into the culture of German families. Neither Steve's nor Richard's families were comfortable to her, although she had loved members of both families, certainly. But there had never been the immediate comfort she now felt on the other side of the world, in the Homeland.

Diane and Joanne got on well from the start. Diane could see they were similar women. Perhaps James was looking for a girl just like Mother, as he called her. Well, there were some differences. Diane had spent years in the business world. Joanne had devoted herself to being a wife and mother. Although, Diane admitted, she felt Joanne could run General Motors. Joanne's family was musical and that was comfortable for Diane as well. Diane knew all about Uncle Jim and his harmonica. His appearances at the Royal Albert Hall were very impressive indeed. Diane knew he had played background tracks for British television. From her vantage point as a once-accomplished flutist, Diane could hear the quality in the melodies of James Hughes. She complimented him at the family gathering. He was humble.

Alfred and Joanne loved the big bands and jazz. Diane brought them the complete set of Glenn Miller, and they were truly overjoyed with the gift. She told them how her parents had danced to the big bands at the Aragon and the Trianon, also at Navy Pier in Chicago. Harry had even died on a dance floor, Diane explained.

Alfred was a gardener and showed Diane his back garden, which was stunning. He had potting sheds, statues, shapes, and forms. He was so proud, and Diane could not believe he did all this work at his age, Alfred being past eighty-five years old. Joanne showed

Diane a photo of Alfred just out of service. He was stunningly handsome. What a lovely couple they had been, Diane thought.

"Alfred has written his memoirs, you know," said Joanne.

Diane was fascinated with them. It was clear neither had settled when they found each other. It was still clear. Here she was arriving at the end of this love story and finding them so admirable, both separately and together.

Joanne spoke with impeccable diction, which is why James spoke as he did. Diane wondered if what James was searching for and had not yet found was the devotion his parents shared for each other. They certainly had not settled.

Diane reflected. The World War II generation had often settled because they were doing their duty. Who was to say they were not right? She thought of Harry and Ione, Laverne and Barbara: two prime examples. At least they had stable lives, which was more than Diane could say, more than her entire generation could say. Still, the unbelievable joy when one is not settling … Diane wondered if she was starting to experience that. Diane's mind wandered back to her first husband, Steve, the father of her children. Perhaps he was right not to settle. God knows Diane had never shown him that she was wild about him. She was young and simply responded to his strong advances. She had expected him to be as self-sacrificial as Harry, and she never really considered that he had needs of his own. Steve was still married to Katherine.

83. Seaside at Torquay
England, 2007
James, Diane

James arranged a week at the seaside, at Torquay. Unprepared for what she would see, the journey through the Cotswolds warmed up Diane's architectural mind for what was to come. She was enamored with both the man and the country.

James pulled up to an old Victorian hotel, explaining that well-to-do Londoners for generations came to the hotel to relax and heal. The woodwork and the detail were spectacular. Diane, with her years in interior architecture, soaked in every detail. Fluting, beading, and Queen Anne arches abounded. There was no elevator, of course, so they humped their suitcases up the wide expanse of stairway to their room. Diane quickly learned that the Brits used that phrase for hauling. James explained that he had used the term "humping" in an elevator in Chicago in 1982 to the complete astonishment of all the Americans there. They laughed as Diane told him about her English friend, John, who was very proper around the ladies. His mistake had been to ask a female secretary for a rubber [eraser] in America.

All the banter proved good foreplay. Diane, finally at age fifty-seven, got the honeymoon she had always dreamed of. They made love before the bags were unpacked, which was not typical of Diane, but she needed the complete abandonment. With Diane, responsibilities usually came first, but not this week. Not the week in Torquay.

After dinner, Diane and James wandered the seaside and came upon a little concert hall. Van Morrison was advertised for that evening, so they bought tickets. After the concert, they walked back to the hotel, arm in arm, like an old married couple. They looked as if they had been together a lifetime. What if, they often wondered, they had talked longer at Marshall Fields in 1982? Diane's answer was always that she was supposed to be there for Richard and Laverne and that James was destined to bring Ellie into the world - if indeed he had. He still did not know for sure.

The week was absolutely blissful, clotted cream, an incredible flutist at water's edge, an elaborate tiled pool in the basement, and the surprise of a wonderful Caribbean restaurant. Diane had been in heaven touring through the Debenhams department store. The splendor of the old store reminded her of the store where Ione worked as a bridal consultant and fitted Diane's first bridal dress.

Diane had never been more comfortable during the early stages of a relationship. The time together with James lacked complications, although she still simmered her thoughts around the apparent damage within him. On Friday night, they found themselves quite hungry and decided to try a place near the water. All week, they had walked past its full length mullion glass windows. Disappointingly, the service was horrible. They sat for over an hour waiting to be served.

Finally, and uncharacteristically, James blurted out, "If they don't hurry up, I am going to tell them to stick it up their bum!"

One of two very proper British, visiting-the-seaside-ladies seated at the table behind James turned around and, looking down her very long nose and chin, said, "I say!"

James could not see her, but Diane could not contain herself. She laughed and laughed, which only caused the old woman to become more irritated. When the food finally arrived, it was also quite disappointing. James apologized, as if all the experiences of the week were his responsibility. Diane explained it was all well worth it and relished the thought that somebody in this world thought she was an irresponsible, shallow woman who laughed at proper old ladies. For years to come, Diane and James would screw up their faces at each other and say, "I say!" and make references to the Torquay Woman. Diane did not hear even one American all week. She surprised people, in fact, when they realized she was not one of them.

For once in her life, Diane abandoned herself in this experience with James. She let herself relax and feel everything he had to give her; it was heavenly. They had toured an historic village and sat in awe in the old church. Everything about England and the Englishman touched Diane's innermost yearnings.

He had loved her for a while from a distance, but this week was his, thought James. He found in her a woman of depth. You could count on this woman. He wondered if perhaps she was capable of bringing out the best in a man. He needed that, more desperately than she knew. James was not the kind of man who would excel on his own, he needed a strong personal foundation. The need was real, but his previous realities had disappointed. There was a part of him that did not want to risk again, but over time, he had been able to think about Diane and converse with her when they were apart. He knew what she had done for her husband Richard, and Laverne following. His hopes had begun to rise, that was for sure. But this week was all about her. He wanted her to relax and just be his for this one week.

London was not anticlimactic after Torquay, to be sure, but Diane would always treasure the week in Torquay in her memories. Diane had back and knee trouble. She wanted to see London from the top of a red double-decker bus and James obliged. Most remarkable was Buckingham Palace, open because the Queen was not at home. The occasion of the sixtieth wedding anniversary of the Queen and the Duke of Edinburgh was at hand. The display of the wedding jewels, crowns, and clothing was over the top.

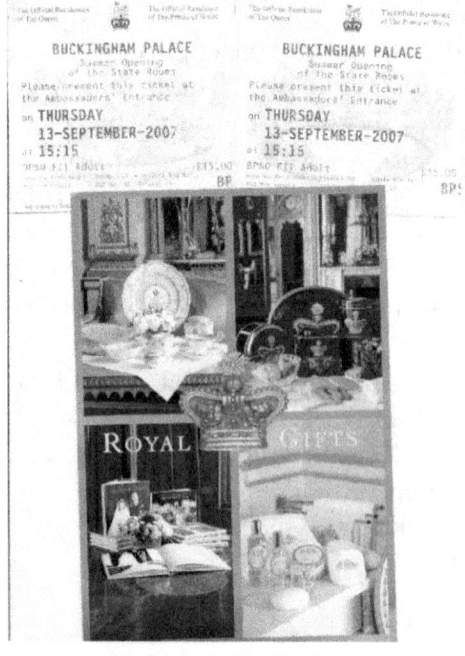

24. Diane in England.

Diane, although a student of interior architecture, was ever so taken aback by the scale of things in the Palace. When all was said and done, James called his mother from the Queen's back garden while Diane took a stroll through the souvenir tents. Lavender hand towels with purple and silver embroidery, for the bath, caught her eye: the Royal Crown embroidered atop in gold, purple and orange, with wedding bells and, "60 Years", all stitched. Diane bought one for Joanne as well.

84. Closing Out
The Lake House, 2008
Diane and James

James quit the advertising agency and took on a couple of independent clients in England so he could travel back to the States, yet keep his flat in England. He and Diane wanted to be together very much, but he would keep a foot in England to avoid putting too much pressure on their relationship. Diane had her home at the lake, but so much had happened there. She did not want to live at the lake house with James and explained the lake location had been strongly associated with her late husband's family, but was not her first choice. She loved New Orleans, where they had met for the second time. It was the city of her heart, and James loved it as well. He went to the lake for two weeks to help Diane clear out the house and prepare it for sale.

Diane tried to be as relaxed as in Torquay, but it was hopeless. At every turn, she saw Richard and Laverne both. She made the best of it, but she and James were both aware of her struggle.

A bar sink make her think of the day she and Richard picked it out. The whole house had been about making Richard comfortable. Richard had been at peace here. She was so glad she convinced him to build it. Laverne, on the other hand, did not care where he was, as long as he was with Diane. His belongings never really permeated the home. But everywhere Diane turned, there were memories of Richard and his family. She knew she had to let go.

Richard accumulated over one hundred thirty Snow Village buildings. Diane had stored them in an area over the lower level Jacuzzi, accessed through an escutcheon hole. Years later, Diane built storage cabinets in front of the hole, with a back cut out to access the storage area. A person literally had to crawl through the cabinet to get out above the Jacuzzi. Diane explained that the items needed to be pushed back through the hole and dealt with. James was game. So, Diane, very awkwardly, crawled through the cabinet and out over the Jacuzzi to her secret storage area. She was going to make war with the *Snows*. She started pushing them through the hole towards James.

She must have been on about Snow Village number fifty when James exclaimed, "Bloody 'ell! How many of these are there?"

Diane started laughing and could not stop. She had not laughed so hard in years. She was literally on the floor and could not stop laughing. When she finally composed herself, she told James, "We're not even half done."

"Well where am I supposed to put them all?" he yelled through the wall and cabinet.

"Just start stacking them on the bed, I suppose," answered Diane with a yell. She tried to imagine what it looked like in the small bedroom on the other side and started laughing again. In the end, Diane gave some of the Snow Villages to the wonderful man who had maintained her home. Sal took quite a few. Diane and James kept five, including the first one. It had been a Christmas present from Ione, and it looked like the old Victorian house that Richard owned when they met. When they were finished, Diane fixed a nice dinner with wine. They deserved it!

Afterwards, she promised to play the flute for him. She played her warm up tune, and James asked what it was. "*Black is the Color of my True Love's Hair*," replied Diane.

"Really?" said James, as he pushed his hand through his own black hair.

85. Caught Up in Oppression
England, 2009
James, Jessie

For James, the sun rose and set on his daughter Jessie. Yet she remained in his ex-wife's hometown in Northamptonshire when he first went to America. It was her choice in the end. Disappointed over Patricia's treatment of her, and a wild teenager at heart, Jessie elected to live with her Mum, Catrine, in a very permissive atmosphere. James' son, slightly disabled as he was, went off on his own and was living with a woman up in Leeds.

Jessie was most like her dad. She had ambition, fire, drama, and liked to laugh. Jessie had not chosen well in the men department. Mother of three children, she recently lost a baby. Her husband was in trouble with the law. James called it, "the plague of Corby." He rued the day he went there to work as a young man and wound up the caretaker of a wild alcoholic. He did not speak ill of Jessie's mother to his daughter's face, but privately considered Catrine to be the vilest woman he had ever known. He viewed the entire town as a sad, sad place to call home, and he hated visiting his daughter there. James prayed Jessie would have the gumption to rise above it. He advised her to divorce. At first she objected, but eventually, Jessie divorced her husband.

86. Back and Forth
New Orleans, 2009
James, Diane

James traveled back and forth between England and America once he and Diane found a nice rental home. Diane was still settling estates and trying to sell the lake house more than five years after Richard's death. She did not want any marriage or house plans for a while.

The rental house sat on the north shore of Lake Pontchartrain. James was wary of New Orleans after Hurricane Katrina. They adopted a lovely Chesapeake Bay retriever named Chester, a Katrina rescue who lived in a shelter for a few years. Chester Barnes, his full name, followed James about closely. The two were quite bonded. As a pup, during Katrina in Gulfport, he swam through a forty-foot swell to save his own life.

Watching him in the pool, teaching Padmé to swim, it was easy to imagine him saving other dogs. Padmé loved to head balls back and forth while standing at the edge of the pool, but she was not a natural swimmer. Once in a while, she became aggressive in her ball bobbing and fell into the pool with a slight look of panic. Her large tiger-like paws would clumsily pound the water. She was not a good swimmer. Chester would jump in and, shoulder to shoulder, show her how to get to the steps.

James knew he had to make things right for himself, but Jessie was upset with his attraction back toward America. She wanted to move to Birmingham and be near him. He still encouraged her to do so. After all, Joanne and Alfred lived there. It could be good for everybody concerned.

New Orleans and the culture of the area fascinated James. In Las Vegas, he had explored voice-over work and wound up hosting British comedy there for the local public broadcasting station. He saw in New Orleans an artist's culture where he could explore more of the activities he loved. Both he and Diane needed a warm climate. She had emphysema. James too struggled with his lungs, as Alfred had for a long time.

James always felt he was holding back a little with Diane. Certainly, he felt scarred by women at this point in his life. After all she had been through, he did not want to overwhelm her. He tried to keep things light and airy. He had less trouble with moving about and starting fresh than Diane had. She was leaving Illinois, the lake, and all her family there for good. But with Sal in New Orleans, James hoped it was good for her. Diane had become more of a homebody now. She said she was tired of business and catering to people, although she took on a few design projects that she could do from home. She was planning semi-retirement in March 2010 when she turned sixty.

James loved the rural aspect of the north shore, but Diane came alive in the city. He spent a lot of time traveling across Lake Pontchartrain to New Orleans, so they found an apartment in the city. The owner agreed to the two large dogs. James was no longer concerned about living there, and Mid-city was attractive to him. He started a non-profit foundation dedicated to voice-over training and activities.

James had never been this happy, but Diane was not happy with apartment life, even though they rented the first floor of a charming home. The economic downturn had hit her hard. The lake house, being resort orientated, would not sell in the disastrous real estate market. It was really a second home and the market had hit bottom. Diane continued to pay for it out of her retirement fund, only to be forced to auction it off for a loss in the end. With what little she had left, she bought a small lot in New Orleans and hoped they could recoup in a couple of years and build a small house. She spent hours designing the house. In addition, James was trying to sell his flat, but its value had gone upside-down in England.

Sal had started a new business for herself, a toxin-free cleaning company. "It's an easy sell," Sal explained. "Much different than selling expensive kitchens. Basically, everybody wants to eliminate toxins from their home and exposure to their children and animals."

She found herself working seven days a week. Diane helped as she could with invoicing, emailing and so forth. Sal's previous experience working for Diane paid off. The new business grew quickly.

87. Summertime
Wisconsin, 2010
Diane, James, Jacob, Kallista, Aaron, Alexandra, Karlin, Janet

Jacob and Kallista had built a large home in Wisconsin for their big family, which included a few animals. Kallista, an introvert, was as soft-hearted towards animals as anybody could be. Alexandra had been animal crazy as a young girl.

In 2005, when Diane met Jacob and Kallista in Paris, Jacob announced his new job with a major player in the software industry. And by 2010, he was doing very well. As fast-thinking as his own father, Jacob's ability to see shades of gray, that and his people skills, were all Harry in Diane's mind.

Jacob's house was situated on a large corner lot. Snowy winter photos were gorgeous. Kallista was gifted at home decoration and everything looked great. Kallista used Diane's desk and furnishings from the Chicago Mart in her home office.

It was great for Diane to see the kids again. They were now fifteen, thirteen and eleven. The youngest inherited her mother's blue eyes, but hinted of Diane in younger years. She was as studious as Diane had been. Diane could see she put herself under pressure regarding her schoolwork, feelings she remembered well. Harry and Ione usually thought something was terribly wrong if Diane brought home a B grade on a paper!

Diane arranged to meet Janet to visit Laverne's gravesite. The two women stood over his grave, next to Barbara.

"Did Laverne and I do the right thing, Janet?" Diane asked.

"Yes, I think you did. I certainly appreciate the quality my kids had from him. But Diane, I am so glad it was you he loved. What if it had been somebody horrible, someone I hated? Thank you for bringing that joy into his life. He needed it. Just knowing that he had some warmth in his life and knowing he did not have to settle for a lifetime of feeling out in the cold … well, that means a lot to me."

Diane could tell Janet was at peace with everything. Tears rolled down Diane's cheeks. She would never be sure they did the right thing in staying apart, but it was done now. And the sacrifice allowed her to be there for Richard. She had saved his life three times, forcing him to go to the hospital, before he finally succumbed to an infection.

88. The Sea Air Again
Gulf Coast, Mississippi, September 2010
James and Diane

James and Diane spent the first night of their vacation in Biloxi enjoying the rooftop pool at their hotel. The next day, Diane took him along miles and miles of white sand beach in their older Jag convertible. James was overjoyed to realize this beauty lay only a short jaunt from New Orleans. Enjoying life, enjoying each other, they continued along the coast then cut across Florida for their ultimate destination, Daytona Beach. College kids were gone, the place was nearly deserted. Diane had booked a beachfront hotel Things were going along well, but neither of them felt very settled. Diane wanted her own home again, a home with James. She felt their life was somewhat transient, and she never did well with that.

"How many times must I reinvent myself?" she wondered.

Jacob praised her resilience, but she was getting older and tired of life not settling in, always changing, James coming and going. Diane hated the apartment, even if it was in the city of her dreams.

James had not seen Diane this happy since Torquay. The seaside always agreed with her. He saw her laughing as waves splashed over her and wished she could always feel this happy. It seemed she lived in the past too much. But today, she was a free spirit again, like in Torquay.

Diane awoke from one of those dreams so realistic that one knows it is more than a dream. Without a doubt, Richard visited her in the moments before waking. He spoke distinctly to her. "Give your all to James."

Diane arose and made coffee. She was shaken. She had not heard from Richard in a while, which actually distressed her. She flipped open the laptop to read some news and then noticed the date. It would have been their twentieth wedding anniversary had Richard lived. Diane started shaking. That's why Richard visited her, to make it clear to her. She cried, choking and crying with emotion.

James awoke and asked, "What's going on, sweetheart?"

Diane told him everything, shaking with a spiritual awareness in his arms.

"Is it time we got married, Diane?" he asked. "Is it time I stop going back and forth?"

She loved him so much. She felt so grateful to have her soul's choice at this late date in life. "Yes," she said, "I think it is."

For the first time, Diane was not settling for less than what she should have, and she was grateful. She realized that Laverne had found her at near retirement age and was grateful that when she found James, he was of her own vintage and available. The older we get, she mused, the ever more difficult it is to bond afresh. Diane felt calm.

89. Wedding bells, One Last Time

City Park, New Orleans, 2011
James and Diane, Jacob and Kallista, Nedra, Hope, William, Sal

It was a lovely family time. Diane's maternal cousins, Nedra and Hope, attended Diane at the wedding. Kallista, always on top of things, had arranged an outfit for herself that was gorgeous and in keeping exactly with the colors Diane had specified, black, white and royal blue. Nedra and Kallista were bride's attendants. Hope and Sal worked on the party at the house. James' best friend in New Orleans, a lawyer named William, worked with Jacob to take care of the groom's side once Jacob delivered his mother to the wedding space in front of a palm tree.

Diane and James had chosen a lovely April day for their wedding in City Park, their favorite place to walk and spend time. They found a semi-private spot near Big Lake. James selected the music, *Nights in White Satin* by the Moody Blues, a Birmingham band they both loved. He and William even surprised Diane with a limo ride to the park.

Jacob was in charge of handling Diane, so the surprise was not blown. Diane could not understand why she was not allowed out on the sidewalk to supervise the car arrangements!

Jacob sighed, "I know, Mom, you like to have a plan."

Diane was concerned about who rode in the convertible, how everybody would get to the park. Jacob shook his head. A successful manager himself, he recognized those organizational skills in his mother. He just wished she would give it a rest once in a while.

Diane said, "Yes, but I can be flexible. I can go to Plan B when called for!"

"Well," replied Jacob, "welcome to Plan B!" He opened the door and there awaited a big white limo to take the wedding party, save William and James, to the park. What fun!

The wedding went off without a hitch. They read vows each had written as the breeze gently warmed the guests. At Sal's house, they signed the official papers as the party began. Diane and James wanted the family to have fun. Everyone partied into the night on Frenchman Street, enjoying the music of John Boutté.

At some point, Nedra and Hope finally said, "You had better take us back to our hotel. After all, it is your wedding night."

Diane and James were not terribly concerned about that, but it was nice of them. They had felt married for some time already. "Still," thought Diane, "it is nice to make it official."

James loved his ring with the blue sapphires and white diamonds in the band. Diane did not like diamonds. Her ring was a pink sapphire, similar to the Princess Diana cut, surrounded by diamonds. Diamonds should always be trim, in her opinion.

Sal did a great job coordinating the kitchen, even though her heart was never in weddings, not until gay people could have full rights to marry as well.[11]

---

[11] At time of publishing, the U.S. Supreme Court has upheld the right of gay people to marry in all fifty States.

90. Brum
Birmingham, England, 2011
Jessie, Alex, Joanne, Alfred

After moving to Birmingham for work, Jessie became engaged to a young man named Alex. She had become a mother at a young age and her three children were older. The children now stayed behind in Corby with Jessie's half-sister to attend school there. Jessie was ambitious and wanted to make her way. She had a business mind, but motherhood kept interrupting her.

With the help of the internet, Jessie and Diane had become fast friends. Jessie often asked Diane for advice, which Diane was all too happy to give, as she knew the situation with Jessie's mother. Diane felt it best that Jessie look forward because her mother, Catrine, may still be drinking heavily.

In reality, Diane was surprised Jessie gave her a chance. Her step-mother Patricia so hurt Jessie that she required strong counseling. But Jessie was a sponge in the mother department. She just needed proper attention.

Once she relocated to Birmingham, Jessie began to visit her grandparents, Joanne and Alfred, and her Aunt Annie, who was somewhat deaf from birth. Jessie adored her grandparents. Alfred was always joking around. Joanne was a tower of strength, and now that Jessie was so nearby, a stronger relationship developed, stronger than before. Diane was determined that between Joanne and herself, the young woman would be properly mothered, even if she was an adult herself. Jessie was also close to her Aunt June, who lived in western Canada.

91. Mardi Gras
New Orleans, February, 2012
Poppit la Fleur, Diane, James

Driving near Miró and Esplanade Avenues, Diane noticed a very small dog prance down the sidewalk, make a 90 degree turn into an adjacent street, remaining on the sidewalk. It was so small and looked much neglected. Diane saw no human nearby when the dog pranced down a side street. She stopped and got out of the car, but the dog was too frightened to come to her. Inquiries provided no clues. Diane could not get the dog to come to her, so she risked driving another block to pick up James. When they returned, the dog was where Diane had left her. James, a bit of a dog whisperer, got down on his soccer-bad knees and crawled to the dog, talking to her gently. Eventually, she rolled over, although she initially nipped at him. He picked her up and they took her home, fleas and all.

"She was heading towards that empty school where the feral pit bull terriers hang out," Diane said. "I just could not let her go there. She wouldn't last the night." It was cold outside for New Orleans as Mardi Gras approached.

Diane immediately fed the dog, then bathed her in flea bath. The little female immediately attached herself to Diane and was the sweetest dog you could imagine. After a few days of feeding and bathing, Diane took her to the vet. The little Lhasa Apso appeared to be young due to the lack of weight. She weighed in at nine pounds.

The vet found a chip in the dog. Diane was heartened that maybe some old lady had lost her dog, but the dog was already pulling at Diane's heart strings. The vet called the registered owner, who hung up. The owner lived on the other side of New Orleans.

"She was dumped!" exclaimed Diane, as she tightened her hold of the dog. The vet explained it was basically Diane and James' problem now. Diane called the owner back. The owner said she would take the dog back only if the dog could be delivered to her.

"Yikes," thought Diane. "No way." Diane looked at her vet. "It looks like we have a third dog; I won't take her back to the same owner who dumped her to die on the streets." The vet worked with Diane to reregister the dog. Despite the fact that her former owner had Diane's phone number, that former owner was never heard from again.

Diane's good friend, Carol, lived in the apartment above. She was also an animal-lover and took to Poppit immediately. The two women had become friends and then discovered they were born a few weeks apart in 1950. Carol struggled with a hip injury, but the two women decided to start taking walks in City Park every morning. The new dog, Poppit, would accompany them. Day by day, the little dog became bigger and stronger – she was gaining confidence. She would not let Diane out of her sight. In no time at all, she had gained weight, increasing from nine pounds to thirteen. Diane and Carol would walk early in the mornings, telling each other stories from their lives as Poppit bounced alongside. The Spanish moss hung heavily from the old oak trees along the bayou, shimmering silver in the morning sunshine. Early morning walks in the oaks' shade were cool and pleasant. The two women were able to increase pace as time went by.

James had been calling the dog Little Poppit. Diane renamed her Poppit la Fleur, and the dog became like a child to Diane. Padmé was elderly now, and she gave Diane a look that said "What?" when Diane held the small dog on her lap. Padmé did not understand that Diane could not put a ninety-five-pound dog on her lap! Chester, of course, was glued to James. Poppit had her own glittery hat with purple, gold, and green feathers for the Mardis Gras, but she shook it off and Chester thought it was a bird! Oh dear!

92. Not Again
Lake Region, May, 2012
Richard Jr., Polly

Diane found out through social media that one of Richard Jr.'s step-daughters, the one he had raised from age two, was posting her anguish on Facebook.

Richard Jr., an avid Harley-Davidson owner, had been on his way to work that morning. A woman in an SUV had made a left turn directly into him. He died at the scene at the age of forty-five. This was the second time Polly had been widowed accidentally. She was strong, but what a blow. Between her kids and Richard Jr.'s from his first marriage, seven children lost a father.

Diane was in shock that he was taken in much the same manner of his father's accident, somebody doing something stupid behind the wheel. Richard would have definitely greeted his son on the other side. He would have advised against surviving in a wheelchair.

Polly and Richard Jr. had owned a restaurant-bar. She would continue the business. Her son had been on his way to the lake that weekend to show them his fiancée's ring. Things at the lake were much different than any of them could have imagined ten years earlier.

93. Car Trip
Wisconsin, Summer 2012
Diane and James, Chester and Poppit La Fleur

Diane and James drove north in the summer to Jacob's house in Wisconsin. Padmé, being elderly, stayed with Sal, but Chester and Poppit La Fleur went along on the car trip. Diane wanted to visit cousins en route, Hope and Nedra, not to mention Magna's stepson Jack, who still lived near Diane's childhood home west of Chicago. Diane loved visiting Jack and Wanda, who were so active, despite their advancing years. Dogs were always welcome at Jack's house, but croquet was no longer even discussed.

Wanda was an extremely organized woman who got up early each day. Diane and James arose to a full breakfast, brimming with fresh berries, cakes, and eggs. It was like a restaurant buffet, and Diane could not believe the trouble Wanda had been to so early in the morning.

"Wanda, what have you done!" exclaimed Diane.

"Oh, it is not that much," stated Wanda, who always seemed to put ten minutes' work into five.

After being so well taken care of, Diane and James continued on to Wisconsin.

What a lovely visit to Jacob's house. It was hot for Wisconsin. Both Karlin and Kallista suffered in the heat. As fate would have it, the Cubs were playing the Twins. Jacob secured tickets and off the family went to Minneapolis. Karlin was obviously hot. She asked her Grandma what quarter it was. Karlin was a straight-A student, but apparently baseball was not her bailiwick. Diane smiled and thought of the times Harry had taken her to the ballpark in Iowa to watch the Quad City Angels play, and tried to explain it all to her.

"They are called innings, dear, and we are at five of nine."

"Oh, said Karlin," shielding her eyes.

Jacob tried to explain the nuances of baseball to Diane in the 1980s, and she understood a bit more, enough to enjoy the game.

Kallista and Jacob owned three dogs. Two additional dogs did create some chaos. Chester, who never had accidents indoors, was discovering the joy of covering Buckingham's scent, which was not a good thing. Poppit could not keep up with Mad-Dog-Madison, but she tried for a while. And then there was Jazzmin, who was an aging Golden Retriever. Kallista and Jacob had been so taken with how well Jedi behaved around kids, they adopted Jazzmin. Jazzmin was terrified, however, of Padmé during her visits to Chicago. Diane and James, indeed, had more grand-dogs, counting Sal's dogs, than they had grandchildren living in America.

Both Alexandra and Karlin were accomplished dancers. Diane cried at their annual recital. Alexandra won a scholarship and the two girls danced a sister dance. A passage door was brought on stage as a prop. Diane got the feeling that Jacob was involved in providing the prop-door and was happy to see it go.

Aaron was very tall now, much like Kallista's paternal grandfather. Diane and James noted that he was becoming more adult, purposefully engaging in conversation in the living room. He had one year left of high school.

Diane and James did not have time to make the one-hour drive onwards to see Janet, but Diane was thinking of both Janet and Laverne while she was in Wisconsin. How could she not?

Motoring back south, James and Diane visited with Diane's all-time favorite clients, Evie and Jack in Evanston. Diane loved their Italianate home and James was quite impressed when they drove up and circled in to the front door. Evie and Jack had been her most loyal clients, through the ownership of four houses, since Diane's arrival in Chicago the winter of 1981-82. Evie, the consummate wordsmith, was quite taken with Diane's English wordsmith. Diane loved showing her work to James in a real-world house. James' original desire was to have been an architect, but it had not happened. Like Diane, life and children had happened. Now they could relax and just enjoy one another and precious friends like Evie and Jack.

94. Baby Girl
England, August, 2012
Jessie, Alex, Hayleigh, Joanne, Alfred

Jessie felt predominately happy. Her family was a bit thorny about another pregnancy, especially the Corby group. There were hard feelings all around. But Jessie, for once, was with a man who cared for her well-being and she allowed herself to be happy. Perhaps she could finally have the family situation she had always wanted. Her pregnancy was high-risk and James worried from afar.

"Pregnancy is a life-threatening condition, Diane," he stated with fervor. "It always has been. I am really worried."

"Try not to worry so much, James," Diane implored. "She will be closely monitored."

"I can't help it, Diane." James paced the small living room at their New Orleans apartment.

James remained restless until the day Hayleigh Ella was born. Finally, word came that both mother and baby were well and he let the air out of his lungs with a long sigh of relinquished anxiety. His final papers from the wedding had not arrived. He could not go to England and it was frustrating

Jessie had named the baby for her long lost sister, Elinor. It still hurt that Patricia had rejected her after Ellie's birth. Jess felt she had been a substitute until the real daughter could be born.

95. Ellie!
The Internet, 2012
James and Diane

James routinely searched the internet for his younger daughter. She would be eighteen years old. Unable to find her while he was in England, the return to his own country had, in the end, led him back into depression.

The search was still frustrating and brought back all the emotions of alienation. That's what Diane called it, parental alienation. That word, alien, it ate at him again. He had escaped the alienation by becoming an alien in a foreign country. Nothing really worked out until he found Diane again and began working through his damage with her. Thank God she really loved him. It was like the balm of fresh sea air they enjoyed near the coast. She understood loss and stress and its effects. He was a fortunate man at last.

In the end, Diane found Ellie. Her name was spelled oddly, but it was her. Was she really his daughter? His heart had always felt she was. Diane saw a strong resemblance.

Both James and Jessie sent messages through social networking. Ellie did not want to be bothered with them. James had expected as much, but it hurt. Jessie could not believe that Ellie did not want to know her own sister. It seemed Patricia had managed to create tentacles of alienation. Jessie felt betrayed anew and found the whole thing very difficult.

Joanne could not understand why any of them bothered. Ellie was not her granddaughter.

96. Final Winter
New Orleans, 2012-13
Padmé

Padmé, stalwart as ever, was stricken with bone cancer. Stoically, she continued her job of guarding the entire family. The vet put her on a dog medicine cocktail to keep her going and was as brave as a dog could be. It would be a miracle if she lived to see Christmas. Diane was already grieving for her dog and her soon-to-be-lost link to Richard.

The brave Padmé even made the evacuation with them when Hurricane Isaac threatened New Orleans. They drove west, all the way to San Antonio and north to Texas Hill Country, to stay with their dear friends, Marsha and Gary. They were such kind people and made Padmé comfortable in the laundry room. In the morning, Marsha found herself alone with the ailing Padmé and gently took her outside for her morning constitutional. Gary and Marsha had grown up with Diane. Marsha and Diane had been journalistic correspondents to the local newspaper together, briefing the community on the high school news. In these later years, the two couples were compatible and became fast friends.

When Diane awoke, she saw Marsha's concern for the ailing dog. "She's coming across to be with you, Richard. Take good care of her," Diane prayed. Diane smiled at the thought of Richard and Padmé prancing and playing on the other side, neither of them limited any longer by legs that no longer worked.

Fresh tears welled up as Diane remembered how much Richard Jr. had loved Padmé as well. They would all be together again. Somehow, she felt Richard had sent Poppit to be with her and to help see her through this time. The little Lhasa Apso was always with Diane and loved to sleep under Diane's computer desk in New Orleans. She now slept next to Diane in the Texas Hill Country while Chester slept next to Stephen in the upstairs guest room. Padmé had not climbed the stairs.

Returning home, James and Diane were elated to find Padmé was still with them for Christmas. They kept Christmas quiet and peaceful for their Queen: Padmé Amidala, Queen of Naboo. After Jedi, Richard had insisted on a female *Star Wars* character name. Just a month earlier, Jacob and Kallista had brought the family down for Thanksgiving. Diane and James invited many for dinner at the crowded first floor apartment. Jacob treated the family to a Saints game. After all this activity, Diane and James were happy to keep a quiet Christmas with their dogs.

Chester was good to the ailing Padmé. They had been buddies for four good years. Chester, the natural swimmer, had helped her in the water.

By the time Padmé was too sick to continue, Poppit had been with the family for almost a year. Finally, the day came. James and Diane sadly took Padmé to the vet for her last journey. The vet confirmed that her vitals indicated the end. Diane and James hugged her and petted her until she had gone to the other side.

After Padmé died, something clicked inside Diane's head. She wanted a change, she wanted to be near water again. Diane began extensive research on properties along the Gulf coast in southern Mississippi. After a long talk with James, they decided to pursue living near the beach. This would mean some travel back to New Orleans for James, but their heart was not in building a house on a city lot in New Orleans. Diane wanted a beach cottage to renovate and was willing to invest the research time to find the right house. She worked hard to sell the city lot for an acceptable price. It was an unusually large lot with trees and she was able to get the asking price.

The coastal towns were still rebuilding in the aftermath of hurricane Katrina. Casinos were investing large dollars in the area. New hotel towers were being built along the coast.

Diane and James fell in love with the historic area near the Biloxi Lighthouse on Beach Boulevard. Diane was becoming fatalistic and believed that when things are right, it was obvious. She believed now in divine guidance. Life would fall into place like shuffled cards when one allowed it to happen.

It was as if the cottage had just been waiting for them to arrive and claim it. The roomy house had been empty for five years and Diane could immediately see its potential. Two blocks from the beach and placed ideally above the flood line, the house was perfectly suited to James and Diane. When Diane found out the house was built the year she was born, she was in love. Diane had been hauling around draperies in a suitcase for over a decade. She had found them in an antique store and fell in love with the 1950s satin draperies. When she realized the five satin panels exactly fitted the north window wall in the sunroom, she was ecstatic, as only an interior artist could fathom. The swimming pool was the icing on the cake. It needed repair, but Diane could see the two of them enjoying laps in the pool. The couple both loved swimming.

Diane's bliss was interrupted by a call from the daughter of her cousin, Sheryl Williams. Diane knew that Sheryl had been in the hospital, but Diane had the impression she was getting better. Not so. Sheryl was rushed back to the hospital and suddenly passed away. Diane could not talk. She had to hang up. Sheryl had been with her when Diane was a baby and again at the moment of Richard's death. She had been so kind, heaven-sent really.

As Diane's first babysitter, Sheryl dealt with Ione calling the house, nervous and inquisitive. Sheryl and Cousin Jo Marilyn had reassured Ione. In reality, Sheryl had run into the bedroom with her hand over Diane's mouth so there was no chance of Ione hearing a cry from Diane! How many times had they laughed about that? What an inane thing to think about at this moment. Diane thought the pain should subside, but it did not.

97. The Move
Biloxi, Mississippi 2013
Diane and James

Three months after the move, Diane and James began to feel like normal human beings. Diane had torn a muscle in her chest lifting books, but not until almost everything was in place. The move was complicated. First, there were boxes and boxes of dishes and china that Diane refused to give up, much of which had belonged to Ione, and some of it to Magna. Diane just had to keep the antique glassware. She wrapped and packed all the pieces. She unwrapped and put each precious item away herself. The dishes filled a large piece of furniture, a built-in that came with the house, plus a hall closet. Diane just could not give up any of it. The pink satin handkerchief box sat next to Diane's side of the bed.

Much of James' personal possessions had been in storage back on the North shore. The movers started there, then moved to New Orleans, then out to Biloxi. Everything was placed according to Diane's pre-drawn plans. They managed to fill up the house. James finally got his large office and studio. There was a luscious sun-room by the pool and Diane designed the sparkling room to look period appropriate, with a hint of British Empire. The celadon-green satin draperies hung across the three windows on the north wall.

Diane had her command center. Her desk occupied the old small dining room, adjacent to the kitchen. She had installed her Aga stove in the kitchen. She was at home.

Sunlight drenched the original living room from the east with a southerly fireplace and mantel.

Diane tapped this for the dining room. Years earlier, she and Richard had purchased a painting at a dog benefit that topped off the mantel. She filled the side wall with British Empire pieces she and James found on Magazine Street in New Orleans. And Diane's crowning jewel, her Kondakova painting overlooking the Seine in

Paris with the Cathedral as a backdrop, she displayed in her office where she could see it all day. It reminded her of sitting in Paris, by the Seine, thinking of her two lost loves, Richard and Laverne.

Both Chester Barnes and Poppit La Fleur were ecstatic at all the room and the fenced yard and pool. There had never been two happier dogs.

By the time the dust settled, Diane's longtime friend Sue was on a plane to visit. It was Sue's birthday, and Diane had planned everything in detail. Diane had booked a guest house in New Orleans for the first night. Then the next day, the day of Sue's birthday, they would go across the Lake Pontchartrain Causeway Bridge and have lunch in Mandeville overlooking the lake. That would give them time to get back to Biloxi. Diane had to pick up the custom birthday cake by 4 p.m., and they would have dinner overlooking the Gulf.

Sue threw a wrench into the works. She just had to stop by the Biloxi wooden beach pelicans to take photos. James went into creative photographer mode, taking shots from many different angles while Diane nervously checked the time again and again. Finally, Sue and James returned to the car and they sped towards the cottage.

Sue was tired and went for a nap while Diane dashed back out the door and motored quickly along the beach to the point. The bakery was still open and the cake ready!

When Sue awoke, she had no idea how a custom birthday cake had made its way to the table. Diane warmed in the glow of her friend's surprise.

The week went by fast; Sue was leaving and telling Diane how much she enjoyed relaxing in their home. She felt she had been treated like a queen. Diane reflected and held Sue in a hug.

"Life is good, Sue. It is right," Diane whispered quietly. "I have not settled."

"I know, Diane, I know." I'll be back next year. Diane watched her go and thought of the night Harry died. Neither Sue nor Steve had been able to console her in the least. Nobody could have, Diane mused. She could no longer see Sue and turned to go home.

98. A Patchwork Quilt
December, 2013
Kallista, Janet, Diane

Kallista felt ready for Christmas – preparing a large house and buying for a family always took time, but she was challenged again this year. She decorated two trees, one each side of the family room fireplace, and maybe there would be one put up on the porch as well. A new fireplace had been built on the porch - it was filled with comfy cushioned furniture, yet a bit rustic. It fit well in Wisconsin.

Kallista's mother-in-law would be visiting right after Christmas. Diane was flying up in awful weather to see the girls' dance competition. Aaron would be home from college.

Kallista ran marathons. She could outrun her husband, but he joined her in some marathons as well. They had been in Boston the previous spring when bombs had changed everything. Kallista ran past the finish line, paced down for a few blocks and was cooling down. Jacob did not run in Boston; but watched at the finish line. Then he too moved up a few blocks toward his wife. When he realized there were explosions, he ran to put his arms around Kallista, knowing she must run away on legs spent from the marathon. Diane had immediately called him. She never watched television during the day, but because of the marathon, she was doing just that the day of the bombing. Jacob reassured her quickly, then they continued moving away. Frightening indeed. Months had gone by - it was time for precious family memories. Kallista was thankful that their family had not suffered bad results in Boston. The bad winter was frustrating for a runner. She tired of running on the treadmill in the basement.

Not far away, Janet stood at Laverne's gravesite. If only she could talk to him, ask him more about his time in Germany. She contemplated. Her father had shown no interest in returning to Europe. Now she understood fully. It was his road not taken, a mix of painful and pleasurable memories. Janet could now see he was a man of duty, whether it was war, business, or marriage. If only she could talk to him about it. She held the Bronze Star in her hand, squeezing it tightly. She would unfurl her hand and stare at it, only to squeeze tightly again as she spoke privately with her father. If only they had really talked when her own life exploded in her face. If only … Reluctantly, she turned and left him, still wishing the piece of stone in the ground could magically speak. She had arranged to meet Diane for breakfast on this frigid morning. Janet would drive an hour for breakfast, but at least she could talk to Diane about these things.

Diane waited at the restaurant. "I feel so alone now that he is gone, Diane," Janet whispered. "Not really alone, but alone in a family sense. Do you think there is any way we could trace Erika's child?"

Diane could see what this meant to Janet. "We will try, Janet, but it will be difficult."

"Oh Diane …" Janet trailed off, "… it could be a wonderful journey."

Diane soon boarded a plane to get back to warm weather at the south coast. She and James were scheduled to entertain Christine and her husband in New Orleans. The four planned to have brunch at Commander's Palace in the Garden District. Diane contemplated these people from her past as she flew. Laverne. Janet. Christine. She thought of the quilt pieces that Aunt Magna had given to Diane, had left in her care. The pieces were loomed and left to posterity by Diane's maternal great-grandmother, Laura Wallace Birchfield. Life was like the quilt pieces, thought Diane. Best to choose and cherish each piece carefully. She thought of Laverne. She thought of Richard. Both so brave. Both so special.

She closed her eyes and saw a vision of Harry singing, "The yellow rose of Texas, she's the only girl for me!" Diane forced herself back to the present. James would be waiting with a big grin on his face.

99. One Last Time
England, Spring of 2015
Alfred and Joanne, James

Alfred slept all but two hours of the day now. Joanne had been by his side over sixty years and had reconciled herself to his impending demise. Lymphoma and Alzheimer's disease were at work on the ninety-three-year-old man. Their love story was almost over. She was as fit as could be expected; worry had stressed her, but she took her medication. She rested more now that Alfred slept so much. But it was lonely. She felt caregivers lost their identity. She talked to June in Canada, James or Diane in America, and her youngest daughter, Annie, would come by. Occasionally, a grandchild or Annie stayed with Alfred, and Joanne would get out for a bit to a special event or shopping. The supermarket made home deliveries, her saving grace. Joanne was smart and adept with a computer, despite her age. She would get online, order her groceries, and they would arrive at her door. Her older brother also struggled with a spouse with dementia; it seemed to be their lot these days. Well, they were strong enough to do it.

Joanne tried to prepare Alfred, as James was about to arrive from America. She asked him if he knew who James was.

"Of course I do! He is my son." Joanne, hearing this recognition, brightened. Recently, Alfred had not known his sister.

James hailed a taxi for the short ride from the airport to his parents' cottage. He had not seen his parents for a very long time. Between post-marriage paper work and a bad knee, his traveling had been curtailed. He knew his father's appearance would be a jolt, and James was, in his words, shattered from the trip.

The hug from Joanne instantly gave him strength. She was so very happy to see him. He did not regret his life in America, but he did regret not being in England for his parents and Jessie.

James was like a special tonic for the ailing Alfred. He really perked up when he saw James. Alfred managed to talk at length with James – about football, most certainly. They both loved the home city team, The Birmingham City Football Club, the Blues.

Alfred complained about his memory and looked worried. James avoided talking about the cancer, as Alfred did not remember he had cancer. James was quite relieved to see the same twinkle in his father's eye as had always been there, as well as his wry sense of humor peeking through the haze of Alzheimer's disease. Joanne endeavored to keep things as calm as possible.

The entire family was amazed. In regard to Alfred, it seemed the clock had been rolled back a bit by James' arrival. Joanne organized a family barbecue and James looked forward to seeing his uncle, James Hughes.

Jessie brought the baby by. She was having minor strokes, and pregnant again. Joanne was not immediately supportive. Joanne felt having so many children held her bright granddaughter back in life. Jessie went to the doctor to find out why she wasn't feeling well and came back with an image of her next child – she was in a state of shock. She shook her head. The wedding dress she had purchased for her June wedding just would not work!

James braced himself for another worrisome pregnancy and arranged to spend a day at Jessie's home with them.

The trip to England ended too quickly. James looked at his parents, feeling it was the last time he would see Alfred alive. He tried to hide his tears, but Joanne was far too observant. He sank into the taxi, rooted in nostalgia. James rubbed his knee and remembered that long walk uphill with his father to the football stadium, then that long walk across the car park and into the grounds where the atmosphere was *electric blue*.

Alfred was exhausted. He went to bed. Joanne could hear him calling out. "Jimmy, I love you. Jimmy, I love you."

100. Old Soldiers
Huntsville, Alabama and Hume, Illinois, 2015
Vern and the Roth Family

Vern Williams was living in a home in Huntsville, Alabama. He was near his grandson, Sully Williams. His younger cousin, Diane would be visiting for their joint March 15th birthday. Diane had been born on Vern's twenty-fifth birthday. That same month in 1950, Vern's first son had been born. Everything had been so new after the war. Life had been good.

How had ninety years gone by so quickly? He frowned, unusual for him. Life felt so spent. His wife was gone, and Rick, his eldest son, had committed suicide a few years earlier. Vernon had started life with a mother, Nellie, who had done the same to him. It did not feel fair at all.

Vern's younger son was arriving from China, where he lived, for the birthday celebration. Stan had made arrangements for a noon-time celebration at the home. Vern was in Huntsville so as to be near Sully, his grandson. Sully and his wife would bring their toddler Sam, the only person to carry on the Williams name in their branch of the family. Harry and Don had fathered a daughter each. Dennis had not lived. With his mother's problems, Vernon had been an only child as well.

Seeing Diane again was a blessing. This celebration was the first time they were together on their joint birthday. Once again, they all talked about the day at Pearl Harbor. Then Vern added, "You know, Harry taught me to drive! He ran alongside while I was driving."

"Why did he do that?" Diane queried.

"There wasn't room for him to do anything else," Vern laughed.

***

Hume, Illinois, Memorial Day, 2015

Roy Roth drove and pondered. He had plenty of family with him. Seventy years had passed since his father, George, lost his life in

Germany. His uncle, Dall Roth, had been killed one day later on the Bridge at Remagen. Roy was just a little boy at the time. Not many years after, he lost his only brother, Donald, due to illness. Roy was happy to have his own long life, to have been there for his mother, Bernadine.

Now the fallen Roth brothers were honored on Memorial Day in their little home town of Hume. Veteran Bob Darlington was in charge. His wife, Maureen, was an English war bride.

Seemingly, the whole town turned out for the celebration, despite a heavy downpour of rain. Roy was informed that some of the Craig family would be in attendance. His uncle, Dall Roth, had been married to Magna Craig. They did not have children, but Magna had so many nieces – perhaps some of them would be there.

Roy spoke at the podium. This day was special, and it reminded him of what he had lost so many decades ago. Lost pieces of family. He had not gone into service himself, much to the relief of his mother. Roy had named his oldest son Donald for his brother. Donald, Roy's son, served twenty-one years in the Illinois National Guard and often spoke of the sacrifices the elder generation had made. Many letters and stories were told of George and Dall, killed a day apart in Germany, their lives cut short, their wives left at a young age.

Now one of Magna's nieces stood at the podium. Her name was Diane, and she was reading a letter written by her father to Roy's uncle Dall. Oh yes, Harry. Roy could remember him from his childhood. Ione was Magna's sister. He remembered them now.

After the ceremonies, Bob and Maureen tracked down the man with the English accent so Maureen could talk to a countryman. His name was James, and his wife had read her father's letter at the podium.

Roy Roth sat down to speak with Diane. They spoke of their common aunt and uncle, Dall and Magna Roth.

Roy looked into Diane's eyes.

"Diane, did you know Dall died on the Bridge at Remagen?" Diane shook her head with a "yes," but could not speak for a moment, for what seemed like a frozen moment.

The Bridge. Laverne and Dall. Lessons in settling and not settling.

Annexes

Main Characters in Illinois and Iowa

Harry, from the Williams family group, married to Ione.

Ione, from the Craig family group, married to Harry.

Dall, from the Roth family group, married to Magna.

Magna, from the Craig family group, married to Dall.

Diane, Harry and Ione's daughter. Her children, born in Iowa and Wisconsin, are Sal and Jacob. Their father, who marries Diane when young, is Steve, who is from Iowa.

Joseph, from the Ertle family group, married to Lillian.

Lillian, from the Volcker family group, married to Joseph.

Richard, Joseph and Lillian's son.

Central Pivotal Characters

Laverne, from Wisconsin, who is with Dall Roth in the Army during WWII, The Bridge at Remagen, and becomes important to Diane in later years.

Janet, Laverne's daughter with Barbara. Janet also has a brother. Janet's children are Jill and Ken.

Main English Characters

Joanne, from the Hughes family, married to Alfred.

Alfred, from the Smith family, married to Joanne.

James, the elder, from the Hughes family, Joanne's older brother.

James, the son of Joanne and Alfred.

Jessie, James' daughter with Catrine.

The Families
Williams Family

Harry is the youngest of seven children. Alice is his mother and John Irvin is his father. He has older brothers: Dennis, Ray, Irvin, and Don. He has two older sisters: Eleanor and Gladys.

John Irvin is the caretaker of the Sconce Estate, named Fairview Farm. There is a pond at Fairview Farm. "Settling" begins at the pond.

Harry marries Ione Craig and serves in the Navy in WWII. Diane is the only child of Harry and Ione. Harry and Ione move to Iowa and finish raising Diane there on the Mississippi River city of Davenport. Diane marries Steve when she is young, but thirteen years later they divorce after having two children, Sal and Jacob. Steve marries his school secretary, Katherine. Diane moves back to Illinois and settles in Chicago, where she later marries Richard Ertle in 1990. But there is more love interest for Diane, both past and future.

Sheryl Williams is Diane's first babysitter and paternal cousin, the daughter of Don Williams. She has a helper with the babysitting, Cousin Jo Marilyn, who is Ray's daughter. Vernon Williams is the son of Harry's older brother, Irvin, and becomes motherless at a young age. Cousin Jack Thompson is Eleanor's son.

The Craig Family (descendants of Palmer Tingley, who sailed on The Planter from London)

Magna and Ione are sisters, two of four. They also had four brothers, but three die young. Their brother, Harold Robert Craig, survives for a few more decades. Their mother is Goldie Irene Birchfield Craig and their father is Jonathan Frank Craig. Magna and Ione marry Dall Roth and Harry Williams respectively, and the two men are best friends. Nedra and Hope are maternal cousins to Diane, Ione's only child. Nedra is the daughter of Ione's younger sister, Golde, and Hope is the first of the next generation, the grand-daughter of Harold Robert Craig. Hope's mother is Shirley Craig Eastin. Cotton is the sister between Magna and Ione in age.

Roth Family

Contribution of material for "Settling" comes from Celena Roth Hyde and her husband, Dan Hyde. Celena is the niece of Dall Roth, a central character in the book. In real life, Dall enlisted in the army in WWII because his younger brother, Glenn (Celena's father), was drafted, as did Dall's other two brothers (George and Harry, "Harold" in the book). Of the four brothers, two died in Germany, and two returned home wounded. In the book, Dall marries Magna Craig. George Roth, who dies in Germany, leaves his wife Bernadine a widow with two children, Donald and Roy. Donald dies young from illness, but Roy leads a long and full life.

Ertle family

Joseph is part of the Ertle family and lives in a huge German settlement south of Chicago. He is a younger child of his father's second family. Joseph is in the army in WWII and serves in the south Pacific. Joseph marries Lillian Volcker and has one child, Richard.

Volcker family

Lillian also comes from south of Chicago and marries Joseph Ertle. She has a much younger sister named Bethany, who is just a few years older than her son Richard, Lillian and Joseph's only child. Richard becomes Diane's second husband, married in 1990. Richard Jr. is his son from his first marriage. He also has a daughter from which he is mostly estranged due to divorce from Mary, his children's mother.

Central Pivotal Character Laverne

Laverne is from Wisconsin and serves with Dall Roth in the 78th Lightning Division in WWII. He has a love affair in Germany, during the occupation, with a German woman named Erika. When he leaves Germany, Erika is pregnant. He just wants to go home and marry Barbara, his American sweetheart. Barbara forgives him for Erika, but she does not know there is a child to be born. Barbara and Laverne have two children, and their daughter Janet becomes good friends with Diane while Diane is living in Wisconsin in the 1970s. But the real story, carried on privately, is the story of Laverne and Diane.[12]

---

[12] Janet and Diane from the story began searching, in real life, in 2014, in Germany, for Erika's child.

Hughes family

Joanne is a young girl in the Hughes family during WWII. She lives in England during the Blitz, and she relies on her older brother, Jimmy (James Hughes). James Hughes becomes a renowned classical harmonica player who records music for the BBC and plays at the Royal Albert Hall in London, England.

Smith family

Alfred returns from serving in the British army in WWII, after sleeping on the Spanish Steps in Rome. He is disillusioned in love, but eventually marries the younger Joanne Hughes. Their son is named after Joanne's brother. Their son, James, at age 56, will marry Diane Williams Ertle, a widow, in America. James has a son (Len) and daughter from his first marriage to Catrine, as well as a daughter named Ellie from his second marriage with Patricia. Jessie, his older daughter, is the apple of his eye. James has two younger sisters, June and Annie.

Acknowledgements

When I think of "not settling", I always think of my good friends, Evie and Jack Forstadt, two of my first Chicago clients. They bought three custom libraries from me over the years, the first in 1982. For years, I have believed their marriage to be the best I have ever seen. And also, then, I think back to the 1970s and remember my dear friend Lea and her husband Sam. I thought the same of them back in those early days in Wisconsin. With special dedication, then, to the late Lea Pastorello and her Sam. Together they wrote a forty-year love story. And as I write, I grieve the most recent loss of Jack Forstadt. When I think of the truly good and admirable people I have had the privilege to call friends, these four stand out. Without them, I would not comprehend "not settling" in quite the same manner.

This book has its own defined life now. I wish, especially, to thank Celena Roth Hyde and her husband, Dan Hyde, today's generation of preservers, for their love of family and history. Celena, the real-life niece of Dall Roth and daughter of Glenn Roth, submitted a full CD of Dall Roth letters and relished every moment of the journey. Pay attention, we learned, to the generation before us as they are dying. They give out valuable information; perhaps even information that surprises.

This book honors our parents. I say our because my husband and editor, Stephen James Smith, has helped me immeasurably with this book. It really is he who has a career as a writer and media professional, but his encouragement to me has been profuse. I have reached back to my journalism days in Iowa to resurrect my own love of writing. And so we celebrate our parents: Harold and Imogene Williams, Albert and Josie Smith. We thank them, although they had no choice, for living so honorably in such an impossible time. And I fill with tears now as I think of my late Aunt Milly, Mildred Craig Roth Schroeder, the magnificent Magna of the book. And of course, a special acknowledgement goes to Uncle Jim Hughes in England. May his music never cease to amaze future generations. Uncle Jim's little sister, my mother-in-law in England, has contributed in ways she does not realize to the writing of this book. Josie Hughes Smith really was a little girl in the Blitz, while my English father-in-law, Albert Smith, now age ninety-three, deserves kudos for writing his memoirs and for being a WWII *Desert Rat* in the first place.

I cannot begin to describe now my relationship with Jill Ramberg, the real life daughter of Roger Laverne "Bud" Ramberg (Laverne in the book). She has shared the living of this book. She has been in the pages with me. She was my son's Sunday school teacher when he was three, and she still talks about his beautiful eyes and curly hair, even though in present day he has no curls. As I write, we are searching for the Erika in the book, hoping to find her child, Jill's sibling in Germany. Jill now wears Roger Laverne's Bronze Star as a pendant, the Bronze Star Roger earned on the Remagen Bridge.

Two wonderful women from a private Facebook page, one of them in Germany, helped us so much. If we do find Erika's child, it will be with their volunteered help. I wish to thank Ursula Braun and Alesandra D'Alì. Others from the town of Grebenstein, Germany, have reached out to help us through email and phone. Thank you to Mr. Rudolph and Klaus-Peter Lange for their attempts to help

I wish also to express thanks to to the late Major Joe Lipsius, who passed away Sept. 6, 2015. He emailed with me throughout 2014 at age ninety-six. He spent time in the little town of Grebenstein. [Visit Joe's website, www.69th-infantry-division.com/Joestuff.]

25. Major Joe Lipsius during the occupation. Sketch by an unknown German artist.

Joe took command of the 311th Regiment in November 1945, when they moved to Bremerhaven, and remained in command until the unit disbanded a few months later. Roger Laverne returned to the U.S. in December, 1945.

A note of thanks to Pastor Gerhard Klein, Grebenstein, Germany, and the American Bishop John Shelby Spong for taking the time to help. Personal friends have cared and listened and read: Marsha and Gary Myers, Ann Prow, Rachele Simmons-Taling, Elizabeth Hallowell and her friend Paul. You have all been so encouraging. Sue Atkinson and Carol McGrath are the ultimate cheerleaders. Special thanks to my number one reader during her morning coffee time overlooking the Pacific, Chris McGuinness. The ever-organized Linda Faust, who plays word games with my husband online, has agreed to be my number two reader. Special thanks to Dr. Bill Hendricks for his help, and for taking me to the prom in 1967. Bill reconnected me to Tom Driscoll, who attended Davenport West High School back in the day. Today, Tom is Managing Editor of Shipwreckt Books Publishing Company. Lost Lake Folk Art is a Shipwreckt Books imprint.

Prior to publishing, four people who are involved and well-read on the subject of the *Lightning Division* helped me with historical authenticity. Special thanks to historian Jeff Stone of Ohio (grandfather: Company M squad leader, 311th) and Ron Wilson of Illinois (father: Carl L. "Tex", Company A, 310th), Jim Cooper of Ohio (father: Company K, 311th) and Stan Adydan of New York (uncle: Raymond E. Hahn, Company E, 311th).

[These people came to help me through my appeals on the website, www.78thdivision.org, and Ron Wilson's Facebook page, 78th Lightning Men WWII, www.facebook.com/78thLightningmenWWII.]

As I neared completion of this book, I received some very impressive help from a German "search angel". Daniela Rode, from the non-profit organization G.I. Babies Germany e.V., has arranged a feature article in the main newspaper of Kassel, Germany, the large town near where the 311th was stationed. An article and photos of Laverne, (Roger Laverne Ramberg) will run in the paper very soon. How Jill and I wish we could have met her there for coffee. Time presses on, and we wonder if we will ever find Erika's child, the child of war and survival.

On Memorial Day, 2015, Stephen and I attended a special service to honor Dall and George in Hume, Illinois. How moving it was! Thanks to veteran Bob Denbo of Hume. And how thrilling to meet Ray Roth, George's son, and his family.

One week prior to publication the 78th Division website yielded a special contact for me. Dallas lawyer Peter Malouf contacted me to let me know his father, Edward Malouf, [13] was alive and well. Ed

---

[13] Based upon the recollections of Edward Malouf, 78th *Lightning Division*, 311th Infantry, B Company, from Dallas, Texas. Ed, who celebrates ninety years of life in 2015, recounted many of his adventures to the author. In the foxhole, he played cribbage. He recalls the crossing of the Bridge at Remagen, remembering the smoke machines most explicitly. He remembers the blackness and crossing the bridge as fast as he possibly could. By the time he rested from the crossing,

was able to make final contributions to me – and what an experience! Ed, a *Timberwolf* in B-company, crossed The Bridge and lived to tell of it. His stories about the medics, like Roger Laverne, brought tears to my eyes. Indeed. Ed went on to serve in the Air Force during the Korean War and is the father of nine children and the grandfather of twenty-three. I am sure they are all proud of him.

Many, many everyday yet ever-important people have contributed to the fabric that I now cherish as **Settling**.

Ed had been awake seventy-two hours. He participated in the capture of Honnef on the east side of the Rhine. In Honnef, he had to fire his M2 mortar only sixty-five yards, but over a building. This required an extreme tilt of the weapon's base plate. Ed continued on to Marburg and Grebenstein, and finally to Bremerhaven. He is proud of the 311th action in the Hürtgen Forest, where they held off the German 6SS Panzer Army. He is proud to have been part of "The Show," as he called the War in Europe. During the Allied occupation after Germany surrendered, Ed participated in a variety program called *Off Limits*.

.